JUST WANTED YOU TO KNOW

A SECOND CHANCE WITH FIRST LOVE SMALL TOWN ROMANCE

MEN OF THE MISFIT INN
BOOK FIVE

KAIT NOLAN

TAKE THE LEAP PUBLISHING

A LETTER TO READERS

Dear Reader,

This book features characters from the Deep South. As such, it contains a great deal of colorful, colloquial, and occasionally grammatically incorrect language. This is a deliberate choice on my part as an author to most accurately represent the region where I have lived my entire life. This book also contains swearing and pre-marital sex between the lead couple, as those things are part of the realistic lives of characters of this generation, and of many of my readers.

If any of these things are not your cup of tea, please consider that you may not be the right audience for this book. There are scores of other books out there that are written with you in mind. In fact, I've got a list of some of my favorite authors who write on the sweeter side on my website at https://kaitnolan.com/on-the-sweeter-side/

If you choose to stick with me, I hope you enjoy!

Happy reading!

Kait

CHAPTER 1

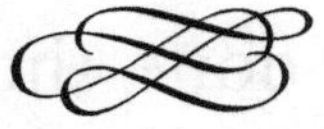

"I can't believe Sam and Griff got hitched in Vegas. Again."

Declan Callahan accepted the beer offered by his foster brother, Mick Routledge, before turning his attention back to the dance floor. The second "first dance" of the wedding reception had just started. "With the sparks they were throwing off at the bachelor-bachelorette weekend a few weeks ago, I'm not surprised. And hey, at least we don't have to sit on the secret of their first marriage anymore."

When that little detail had emerged among the brothers during Kendrick's bachelor party, Griff had sworn them all to secrecy. All he would say was that he'd screwed things up with

Samantha Ferguson the first time they'd impulsively married at twenty-two, and he wanted to make it right. Apparently, the events involving the wedding party that had thrown them back together again—and whatever adventures they'd gone on after—had done the trick. Their newly hitched status had been revealed a little earlier, when Griff refused to come down for the garter toss, and both Kendrick and Erin—the actual bride and groom—had insisted this reception be a celebration for all of them. Hence the *second* "first dance."

"They look happy."

The wistful tone in Mick's voice had Declan looking back at his brother. "They do. You feeling the single this weekend?"

"Aren't you?" Mick countered.

"I mean, yeah, but I was feeling the pinch long before this wedding." It was a discomfort so familiar, he seldom noticed it anymore.

"When was the last time you had a date?"

Declan huffed a laugh. "That was a couple of presidents back."

Mick's eyes widened. "Seriously? Dude. *Years?*"

A little self-conscious, he jerked his shoulders in a shrug and tipped back his beer. "It's not like I've got a hell of a lot of time or bandwidth to even think about dating. Single parenting is not for the faint of heart." And after the number his ex-wife had done on him, his ability to trust wasn't exactly undamaged.

"Fair enough. But look around. All four of our sisters are married with kids. Griff and Kendrick are both married. Hell, even Kyle finally got his head out of his ass and fixed things with Abbey, and she looks so pregnant, I'm half afraid she's gonna go into labor right here. Doesn't all that make you feel like you're getting left behind?"

Could you be left behind when you were the one who'd done the leaving in the first place?

Declan couldn't stop his gaze from seeking out Abbey Whittaker. Well, Keenan now. He'd been keeping tabs on her location since he saw her in the church for the wedding earlier, mostly so he could steer clear. Not that he didn't like Abbey. It was more out of fear of the questions she'd inevitably ask—the ones he didn't have good answers to—and the tongue lashing she'd been sitting on for twelve years. He one hundred percent deserved that dressing down for how he'd handled things with her cousin Livia all those years ago, but that didn't mean he'd deliberately invite the opportunity.

Ignoring his brother's question, he subtly

shifted the conversation. "The family is growing. You know nothing in the world would've made Joan happier."

"True that. God, I miss that woman." Mick held up his longneck for a toast.

"We all do."

Joan Reynolds had been a force of nature. A foster parent for more than twenty years, she'd managed to build a massive extended family with unshakable ties that had lasted beyond her unexpected death in a car accident a few years before. As a single dad, Declan wanted his daughter to be surrounded by the love of that big family. And he wanted the comfort of knowing people he trusted were nearby and had his back. It was why he was finally coming home.

Out of the corner of his eye, he spotted Abbey and Kyle migrating in their direction. A low-level panic had his gut clutching. Time to vacate the premises.

"I'm gonna go track down my spawn to make sure she isn't getting into any trouble. Catch you later, bro."

He bumped Mick's fist and set off for the perimeter of the reception. People were everywhere. Music and conversation filled the cavernous space of the Eden's Ridge Artisan Guild and Education Center. The brainchild of his sister Maggie, and her husband Porter—yet another of his foster siblings—the Guild was home to far more than a maker's space and the artisan market showcasing craftspeople from around the region. This part of the building, which had been converted from an old lumber mill that Joan's great-great somebody or other had built, was frequently used for events, like tonight's wedding reception or the weekly Jam Nights where local musicians gathered during the cold months. There was more classroom space upstairs and workshops on the floor below. He hoped like hell Scarlett hadn't gotten into any of those. She was curious as a magpie, a trait which could get her into all kinds of trouble. But at least it was less trouble than she'd likely get into on her own at the Harvest Festival carnival they were missing because of the wedding.

He didn't have to go far. He spotted his daughter shoulder to shoulder with his sister Athena's boys, Dylan and Jesse, stalking the cake table. If she had more than one piece, what was the harm? A bit of a bellyache? It wouldn't hurt her to learn her own limits there.

Satisfied she was safe, Declan wove his way through the crowd and found an open spot at one of the tables at the periphery of the room. Shrugging out of his tux jacket, he finally popped his tie, shoving it into a pocket and unbuttoning his cuffs and collar. They were well done with proper pictures. He deserved the chance to actually relax. He was contemplating a second beer when Maggie dropped into the next chair.

"You're not going to be able to avoid her forever once you actually start your job as manager of this place."

"Avoid who?" But he knew, even as she arched one blonde brow and fixed him with that I-see-through-your-bullshit stare she'd mastered as a corporate attorney in Los Angeles.

"Abbey."

Yeah, that was something he hadn't really thought about when she'd offered him the position a couple of weeks ago. In the grand scheme of things, it didn't matter because the job was perfect, allowing him to come home and keeping the business in the family, as Maggie wanted.

Knowing better than to continue pretending ignorance, he dropped the act. "Yeah. I know."

"Might as well bite the bullet."

"Not yet. Not here, anyway."

She leaned forward. "Do you really think it's gonna be that bad?"

"I don't know. Maybe. I figure she's going to interrogate me about everything that happened twelve years ago, and she's not anywhere near as gentle and sweet as her cousin. I know she was pissed how I handled things. Or didn't."

"Sure she was. But she got educated."

Of course, *someone* in the family would have told her. Abbey was friends with all his sisters, married now to one of his brothers. He was an idiot not to have thought of that before. Declan wondered if she'd ever told Livia what had happened. Why he'd effectively ghosted her.

The memory of it made him cringe and automatically reach to loosen the collar that was already loose. That whole situation was one of his greatest shames. He'd been thinking about it, thinking about *her,* almost nonstop since he'd come home for the bachelor-bachelorette weekend, because the last time he'd spent any significant time in Eden's Ridge was that summer when they'd been together. When the world had been nothing but a big ocean of possibilities. Before Bridget and the bomb that changed the course of his entire life.

Realizing Maggie was still staring at him expectantly, he cleared his throat. "I'll work my way up to it. But not tonight. Tonight is all about celebrating."

And if his sister's gaze called him a chicken shit, well, he was good at pretending not to see things.

* * *

AT THE FAMILIAR scents of grease and cooking meat, Livia Applewhite felt a few layers of stress melt away. After the day she'd had, she *needed* this girls' night out with her two best friends. And definitely a slice of Mama Pearl's famous coconut cream pie. Maybe before dinner. Spotting Autumn and Riley in a corner booth in the back, Livia made her way across the black and white checkerboard tile floor of Dinner Belles Diner, offering nods and waves to other patrons she knew along the way.

Autumn shoved a glass in her direction as she slid onto the seat. "You look like you can use this."

"You are a goddess." Livia took a long pull on the Diet Coke and sighed as the sharp fizz hit her system. "I don't know why I thought this was the year to curb my habit."

"Because you vowed you wanted to use my

wedding as an excuse to get healthier," Riley pointed out.

"Seemed like a good idea at the time." And, okay, she *did* generally have more energy now, between cutting back on her Diet Coke habit and doing yoga daily with her sister-in-law, Tara. But some days, she just needed a fix. "Have y'all ordered?"

"Nope. We were waiting for you." Autumn grabbed a menu. "I say we get some grease- or carb-laden appetizer to start, while you share whatever Mitzi did that put that look on your face."

"That obvious?"

"Please. I may have been gone from the library for a while now, but I haven't forgotten her Reign of Terror."

The three of them placed their orders, and over a large basket of onion rings Livia vented about her boss to the one person who could fully appreciate her irritation.

"I've put up with having more work simply because I'm the institutional memory. I've tolerated all her favoritism toward Tricia, even though you and I *both* know she got your old job as head librarian entirely through nepotism by being

Mitzi's niece. And mostly it's been… fine. But today she crossed a line."

"Like changing out the breakroom coffee creamer for laxatives kind of crossing a line, or steal her keys and hide a partly open can of tuna under the seat of her car kind of crossing a line?"

Livia and Autumn both turned to stare at Riley.

"What?"

"Since when did you develop such a finely tuned sense of revenge?" Autumn asked.

Her grin widened. "Never, actually. I'm thinking of the pranks Liam and his brothers pulled when we were kids. Cruz, in particular, was a real hellion. After the stories you two have shared about Mitzi, it seemed some more radical tactics might be necessary. What did she do?"

"She basically threw down in public and refused to allow me to read the book I'd chosen for story time. As if a book about two male penguins adopting a baby of their own to make a nontraditional family in a zoo was some kind of sacrilege. *I* am the children's librarian! It's *my* choice what books to showcase. And it's my right to expand the minds of my audience with stories that reflect the broader world in an age-appropriate manner."

Autumn groaned. "Mitzi and her censorship. It's such bullshit."

"It *is*. And maybe it would be one thing if patrons had complained. But they haven't. In fact, we've had requests. But because it doesn't fit in her narrow window of what she considers acceptable, she's trying to say no. She actually told me I had to get her approval before reading anything off her official list of 'acceptable' titles."

"Betting there's nothing on that list published in the last twenty years." Autumn dipped an onion ring into her vanilla shake.

Livia paused, one brow raised. "Did you just… eat vanilla shake on your onion ring?"

Riley gasped. "Are you pregnant again?"

Autumn laughed. "No. Judd and I haven't finished recovering from the sleep deprivation of Ellie's first year yet. It's just one of my pregnancy cravings that never went away. Try it. It's delicious. Like an elevated version of french fries and a Frosty."

Livia wrinkled her nose in disgust. "I'm gonna go with no."

She stuck another one in her mouth and made mmm noises. "Don't know what you're missing. Anyway, that all seriously sucks, and I'm sorry my leaving left you without an ally in this."

"It's not like Mitzi gave you a choice when she fired you. But I won't lie and say I don't miss having you around. There are some days I wish she'd just get it over with and can me, too. Except I don't have a secret career as an indie author to fall back on like you did, and I have no idea what I'd do instead. I just feel… stuck. You know? I am definitely not where I thought I'd be at this point in my life."

They paused as Mama Pearl, the heart, soul, and opinionated owner of Dinner Belles, came by to deliver their meals.

"Well, child, it's never too late to reinvent yourself. You don't like where you are? Change something."

Livia knew Mama Pearl was right. But that was a lot easier said than done. She wasn't a woman to strike out on her own without some kind of plan.

"You know what would help that self-contemplation? A piece of your coconut cream pie."

The old woman's teeth flashed white. "Ain't nothin' my pie can't make better. I'll bring it along shortly."

"Are you really thinking about some kind of major change?" Riley prodded.

"I don't know. Maybe? I've just reached a

point where I know I can't keep doing what I'm doing. I'm not happy at work." She wasn't happy in her personal life either, but saying so in front of the two of them felt a little too much like sour grapes. Not for one moment did she begrudge Autumn for her marriage to Judd, or Riley for finding the love of her life in Liam Montgomery. They both deserved all the happiness in the world. Livia just wished she'd found a piece of that herself.

Over the course of the meal, conversation shifted to wedding talk.

"I'm so glad we were *finally* able to set a date. It took forever to find one where both Cruz and Jack could get leave to come home for the wedding. After all this waiting, now it's a bunch of go go go! The end of January can't get here soon enough."

"Aren't Liam's brothers still single?" Autumn asked.

"As far as we know."

When they both turned speculating gazes in her direction, Livia pointed at each of them. "No. Whatever you two are thinking, just no. Do not try to match make me with his brothers. I don't have the temperament to be a military wife or girlfriend."

Autumn's grin held a wicked edge. "Doesn't mean you couldn't have some fun for the duration of their leave."

"Says the steamy romance writer."

Livia preferred not to think about how long it had been since she'd had that variety of fun. Not that she objected to sex. She just wasn't great at short-term entanglements. For better or worse, she needed that emotional connection. And hot as Jack and Cruz Montgomery might be—and she had no doubt they'd improved since high school —there'd just never been that connection with either of them.

"Maybe you'll find someone more to your liking in Tennessee," Riley teased.

"I'm going to Eden's Ridge to visit Abbey, not to find some kind of booty call."

"More's the pity. You could do with having your world rocked."

Livia fixed Autumn with a flat stare. "In all seriousness, I need to figure out my life. Namely, what the hell I want to do with it. I'm hoping that getting out of town, away from the job, away from the farm, away from all of my normal, will help give me some perspective."

Autumn lifted her glass. "To perspective."

The three of them toasted.

After their checks were paid, they walked out together.

Riley's hug was extra tight. "I'm gonna miss you."

"I'll be home in two weeks."

She stepped back. "I don't know. It just feels like more, somehow."

Livia rolled her eyes. "It's a vacation. That's it. A long overdue one. Seriously. Just two weeks. I certainly can't leave my brother alone for the first season at the tree farm without Mom and Dad."

She hugged Autumn and stepped back. "Hi to your menfolk and kisses to the munchkin from Aunt Livia. I've gotta get on home. I have an early start and a long drive tomorrow."

With one last wave to her friends, she crossed to the town green, headed for where she'd left her car a couple of blocks down. The route took her by the fountain for which Wishful was named. According to local legend—and widely advertised by their city planner, Norah Crawford—wishes made in the fountain, fed from nearby Hope Springs, came true. Just last week, Livia had given in during a fit of ennui and wished for a love that would last a lifetime. As she strode past the burbling fountain, she nearly stopped again, wondering if making the same wish more than once would increase the odds. A small treasure trove of coins glimmered beneath the water's surface. How many of them had gone unanswered?

Most, she was willing to bet. Maybe they were silly wishes. Impractical wishes. Irrational wishes. Selfish wishes. What was the likelihood that such things actually worked? Truly, it was a foolish thing to give your life over to the whim of wishes. There were countless fictional accounts out there, cautionary tales to be careful what you wished for. She had no idea how a wish for love could backfire, but God knew, if there was a way, no doubt, she'd find it.

No. Better to be the author of her own life, whatever that looked like, than to waste another coin. She just hoped this trip gave her some answers.

Leaving the gurgling fountain in her wake, she headed for her car.

CHAPTER 2

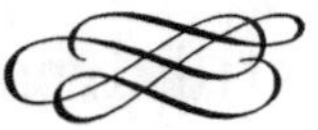

The general story of Declan's life was one of bad timing. He'd been born too soon to a girl who hadn't been ready for motherhood. He'd missed the line drive in the critical championship game that might have landed him a full-ride baseball scholarship to college. He'd met the woman of his dreams mere weeks before the woman of his nightmares permanently altered his life. He'd been five minutes too late to meet country legend Garth Brooks at a hardware store in Nashville several years back. And he woke up with a vague hangover ten minutes too soon the morning after Kendrick and Erin's wedding.

Not that he'd known that as he'd shuffled

down the stairs of his sisters' inn on a quest for coffee.

Not until the explosion hit him full in the face.

For long seconds, he stood on the landing, watching the sparkly cloud drift to the floor, wondering if he was still dreaming.

The grit on his tongue disabused him of that notion. As did the muffled giggles from somewhere below. Recognizing at least one of those giggles, Declan squinted through the glitter haze. His eleven-year-old daughter stood to one side of the stairs, both hands covering her mouth, the hazel eyes she'd gotten from him peeled wide with some combination of mirth and horror. Her sixteen-year-old-and-totally-should-have-known-better cousin, Ari, stood on the other side, her lips rolled in.

"Really?" His hands moved automatically, signing the word in case there was too much glitter still in the air for Scarlett to read his lips.

Her fingers flew in response, though she was looking at Ari as she said, "I told you we should have gone with confetti."

Breaking his paralysis, Declan came the rest of the way down the stairs. "Just… why?"

Ari didn't quite pull off the totally innocent expression. "We were expecting Kendrick and

Erin. It was supposed to be a congratulations-on-your-marriage-and-have-fun-on-your-honey-moon surprise."

He wiped at the glitter now coating his tongue. "You're a bad influence."

Neither girl appeared remotely repentant.

The sound of footsteps and luggage bumping down the stairs had them all looking up, where the bride and groom in question were descending.

"What the…" Kendrick stared at the silver and pink explosion on the stairs.

Erin was the first to spot Declan. Her laugh popped out like a champagne cork. Her husband joined her, nearly bending double with full-on guffaws. Declan just stood, patiently enduring their hilarity and wishing desperately that he'd waited just ten minutes before coming in search of coffee.

The kitchen door swung open. "What's so funny? Oh my God." Ari's mother, Pru, definitely hit more of the horror end of the reaction spectrum. As she and her husband were the ones who actually lived on site at The Misfit Inn, no doubt she was imagining exactly how long they'd be finding glitter on the premises.

Kendrick set his suitcase aside and thumped

Declan on the shoulder. "I gotta thank you for taking one for the team, brother."

"Right. Because this was entirely on purpose."

His brother pressed a fist to his mouth, but more laughter spilled out, anyway. "Oh, man, you're gonna have glitter stuck in your beard for weeks!"

Scratching at his cheek, Declan noted the silver and pink falling from his face like sparkly dandruff. "I may have to shave it."

"That would be an improvement," Scarlett insisted.

His daughter had definite opinions about his facial hair. None of them were good. Reaching out to hook an arm around her neck, Declan pulled her in for a noogie, mindful of her hearing aids. "Brat."

She squirmed, so of course he hugged her extra tight to transfer as much glitter as possible.

"Holy Mary, mother of God." Ari's dad, Flynn, let his Irish out as he came into the foyer and caught sight of his eldest daughter's handiwork. "I don't want to know."

Mick stumbled out of the family lounge, where he'd been dumped on the sofa with a pillow and blanket after last night's reception. His brown hair stuck up in every direction, and his eyes were bloodshot. Given the level of happy drunk he'd been by the end, that wasn't a surprise. He tromped through the glitter before anyone could stop him.

"Well, shit."

"Looks like we missed all the excitement." Griff skirted the mess on the stairs as best as he could, Sam sticking close behind.

"Okay, okay, we've really got to go. Mr. Teague, we have a flight to catch," Erin insisted.

"You're absolutely right, Mrs. Teague." Kendrick pulled her in for a smacking kiss.

Hugs were passed out—everyone avoiding Declan—and then the newlyweds were out the door and headed for Knoxville to catch their flight.

"Okay, girls." Pru clapped her hands. "Vacuum this mess up. It may be all family this weekend, but we're back to normal business tomorrow, and I don't want to see a spec of glitter."

As a chorus of groans sounded from the girls, Flynn nudged Declan toward the kitchen. "Coffee. You definitely need coffee."

"True story." Shaking and brushing off as much glitter as possible, he followed his brother-in-law back to the spacious kitchen with the enormous farmhouse table where he'd eaten countless meals with his foster family growing up.

It still didn't feel quite right without Joan at the head of it. Declan wished he'd been home to see her more before the accident, but he'd been struggling with single parenthood of a special needs child, and his whole focus had been on making sure Scarlett was taken care of. Still, her shadow loomed large in the enormous family she'd left behind, from the four daughters she'd formally adopted, to the countless foster kids who still considered this home.

He headed up the queue for coffee, pouring himself a massive mug and adding a liberal splash of cream.

"If you want to go up and change after you finish your coffee, we can get your clothes washed before you leave," Pru offered.

"Leave?" Sam blinked. "I thought you were here for the week."

"I am. Scarlett's going to be visiting with her grandparents while I sort out the logistics of our upcoming move. I'm dropping her off in Knoxville tomorrow. And I thank you, Pru. I'd just as soon not show up to my ex-wife's parents' house looking like something out of *Showgirls*."

Aware of Sam exchanging a meaningful Married People look with Griff, he felt a frisson of unease. "What?"

Sam waved him to the table. "Well, it's just that I was talking to Abbey at the reception last night. Your old flame gets into town today."

Declan was glad he didn't have a mouthful of coffee. He'd have sprayed everyone at the table at that bomb.

"Livia?" He didn't know why he was asking. It wasn't like he had another old flame who happened to be Abbey Keenan's cousin.

Griff settled onto the bench beside Sam. "Yeah. After what you said at the bachelor party, we thought maybe you'd want to know."

Too much hard cider during the celebratory bachelor bonfire had led to a walk down memory lane he'd been avoiding for more than a decade. He'd been working at Abbey's family's apple orchard for the summer. Livia had been eighteen, all long, tanned limbs and sweetness, and he'd taken one look at her and fallen ass over teakettle. Just the idea of seeing her again had everything in him softening. It had been twelve years since he'd last been graced with that smile. Twelve years since he'd kissed her.

Twelve years since he'd disappeared on her without a word.

Guilt squashed the bloom of softness in his chest. "Even if I didn't already have plans this week, she's not going to want to see me."

Sam laid a hand over his and squeezed. "Hey, if anybody understands what it means to clear the air after a lot of years, it's us."

That was true enough. And yet, faced with the prospect of actually seeing her again, Declan didn't know if he had the stones to actually do it.

"This is your shot, man," Mick added. "If nothing else, you can finally give her that apology you've always wanted. You never know what might come of it. Even if it's just closure, isn't that worth it?"

Would it be worth it to get that regret off his heart? He hadn't thought about a real relationship with anyone since he'd split from Scarlett's mom years ago. And, yeah, part of that was guilt over how he'd handled things with Livia. He had absolutely no expectation that an apology at this late date would truly fix anything. She'd been an amazing girl, who'd no doubt grown into an even more amazing woman. The likelihood that she was even single was slim to none.

But maybe it would be worth facing her for a chance to get rid of the shame he'd carried about it all these years.

Reaching for one of the biscuits in the basket Flynn placed on the table, he conceded, "I'll think about it."

*　*　*

"OH MY GOD, you're finally here!"

Livia stared as her cousin waddled carefully down the front steps of the big white farmhouse, leading with her enormous baby belly. Abbey's husband Kyle trailed behind, hands outstretched, clearly prepared to leap and catch her if she fell.

"Holy crap, Abs! Are you sure there's only one baby in there?"

Abbey rubbed the belly with a laugh. "We're sure. Believe me, I had them check."

Livia carefully wrapped her cousin in a hug, twisting to make room for the baby belly. "Are you sure you still have six weeks to go?"

"So they keep telling me. I'd be completely okay if our beloved little freeloader decided to come early. I am beyond ready to have my body back."

Kyle looped an arm around her waist. "As long as he waits for at least another month. Porter said it's gonna take that long to finish the addition on the house. Neither one of us wants to deal with trying to manage a newborn with construction going on."

"Fair point."

Livia didn't miss how her cousin leaned into him, the picture of contentment. She ignored the stab of envy. It had nothing to do with the fact that Abbey had landed Country Music's Captain America. The two of them had been friends long before he exploded on the music scene, and they'd lost an entire decade together because of someone else's lie. If Kyle hadn't accidentally blurted out that they were engaged on a national TV interview at the end of his last tour, he'd never have come home and been forced to face her. But they'd worked things out at last, and Kyle had overhauled his career as a country music star to better fit the life he wanted with his bride. They weren't wasting a second getting started on that life. Livia was thrilled for them both, but God, she wished there was some prospect of the same on the horizon for her.

Her gaze skated out over the orchards, back to that last summer she'd spent here, when she'd thought things would turn out differently. Back-lit by the cotton candy sky of sunset, the rows upon neat rows of apple trees, stretching across the rolling hills and on toward the mountain beyond, made a hell of a picture. It was a different kind of beautiful from her family's Christmas tree farm back home, but no less a testament to the broader family's commitment to nurturing and preserving the land. The view soothed the ragged edges of the discontent that had dogged her on the nine-hour drive from Mississippi.

It had been so long since she'd spent any time up here. She'd come up for Abbey's wedding back in the spring, but that had just been a quick weekend trip. They hadn't actually gotten to visit. Livia had missed the hell out of Abbey since she'd moved home almost three years ago to help care for her grandfather, who'd been diagnosed with dementia. So when Abbey had invited her up for a visit, she'd jumped at the opportunity to catch up with her favorite cousin and the rest of this branch of the family.

The rest of that family was spilling out of the big white farmhouse. Uncle Mark, Aunt Faye, and Great Uncle Roy. They passed hugs all around, talking over each other, cracking jokes, asking about her trip and the family.

Uncle Mark cut through the hubbub. "We're gonna put you over at Abbey and Kyle's. We thought you girls would want an easier time visiting."

Livia glanced at the house set past the barn. Originally the house where orchard employees lived, the whole thing had seen a massive facelift, with additions going both out and up an entire second story. There was still evidence of the on-going construction, but it was clear the process was nearly finished.

"Oh, that's lovely. Thanks."

"Come on in," Aunt Faye urged. "Supper's almost ready. Kyle, why don't you take Livia's car and scoot it over by y'all's place? You can run her bags inside and come back here."

"Yes, ma'am." Kyle accepted the keys Livia tossed him and went to do as ordered.

Aunt Faye hustled her into the house and back to the kitchen.

As the scents of grease and carbs and baking things wrapped around Livia, her stomach gave a massive growl. "Oh my Lord, that smells amazing!"

"I remembered that chicken fried steak was one of your favorites."

"I appreciate it." Even if she would have to take some extra long walks to make sure she still fit into her bridesmaid's dress for Riley's January wedding.

"It's the least we can do, what with you

helping out with the Harvest Festival this week."

Uncle Roy pressed a hand to the side of his mouth and offered a conspiratorial whisper. "What she's not saying is part of your job will be to distract General Grumpypants over there."

"I heard that, Granddaddy." But there was no heat in the censure as Abbey leaned over to press a kiss to his weathered cheek. "He's not wrong. I'm grumpy as hell because I can't *do* anything with this belly. I'm bored out of my mind."

"I keep telling her to enjoy this part," Aunt Faye admonished. "Once the baby gets here, there won't be any slowing down."

"At least my ankles won't be the size of an elephant's."

"Your ankles are beautiful," Kyle corrected as he rejoined them.

Uncle Roy chortled. "Nice save, son."

They loaded their plates and took seats around the long table.

"How is everybody?" Uncle Mark asked. "I saw Owen post pictures from their latest stint in Arizona."

"Mom and Dad are doing really well. Taking this year to RV around the country has been great for them. They're seeing all the things they didn't have time to see because they were managing the farm. And Dad got a clean bill of health at his last check-up with the cardiologist."

"And your brother?"

"Jace has taken over the farm like he was born to it. Which, basically, he was. That's been another big load off Mom and Dad."

Aunt Faye passed the mashed potatoes. "What about that sweet wife of his? Any talk of bringing along the next generation?"

Livia laughed, imagining the look on her sister-in-law's face if she heard that. "Tara's still only twenty-five. She's not in any hurry, especially since her little brother, Austin, is in high school now, and Ginny's coming up right behind. The two of them really help make up for the lack of grandkids."

Livia and Jace had been exceptionally thankful for that since Tara had come into their lives a few years before. She'd taken custody of her two younger half-siblings when she'd been only twenty. They'd been a delightful addition to the family.

Uncle Mark forked up a bite of lima beans. "Never thought the baby of the family would get married first."

Livia didn't let her smile drop. He didn't mean it the way it had come across. But she still felt the sting. Hard not to when she daily faced the evidence of her baby brother's married bliss.

"What about you, Livia?" Aunt Faye asked. "Any sweethearts in your life?"

She'd been expecting the question. It was standard fare from women of a certain age, particularly those with grandchildren on the brain. But it was a fight not to grit her teeth.

"Nope. I'm pretty sure I've exhausted the shallow dating pool in Wishful. My friends have caught all the good ones." She said it with a laugh, but there was a grain of painful truth to the statement. It seemed everyone around her was happily coupled up.

"That Callahan boy's sweet on you. Ought to do something about that." Uncle Roy sipped at his sweet tea, like he hadn't just made an entirely outrageous statement.

Livia opened her mouth, but had no idea what to say to his proclamation. She hadn't seen Declan in twelve years. Not since that last summer. Abbey had warned her that Uncle Roy periodically got trapped in the past, but somehow Livia hadn't expected this flagrant reminder of exactly the ghost she'd been trying to avoid.

"Livia is here for a *girls' trip*, Granddaddy," Abbey interjected. "Don't you be trying to palm off my favorite cousin before I've gotten my visit in, or I'll enter the pie-eating contest and give you some competition."

"You couldn't beat me. Nobody can eat more apple pie than I can."

"I'm eating for two, old man."

Their friendly bickering shifted the conversation away from the past, but it was too late. His name had been mentioned, and Livia spent the rest of the meal trying not to think about the first love who'd broken her heart.

CHAPTER 3

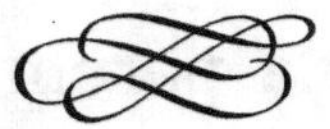

*D*eclan had showered and washed his face half a dozen times. There was still fricking glitter all in his beard. Damn it. Hauling out the beard trimmer he'd only packed to neaten things up before the wedding, he resigned himself to his fate. He really was going to have to shave. He refused to go entirely clean shaven. That was too big a pain in the ass to maintain. But he dialed the trimmer to a couple clicks away from the closest setting and went to work. With every swipe of the blades, it seemed as if he was carving off years.

Fifteen minutes later, he stood staring at his reflection, rubbing a hand over the jaw he could now clearly see again. He'd had a full beard since

Scarlett was born. Seeing this much of his face was just plain weird. He looked different. Younger, except for the lines around his eyes that announced to the world he'd seen way too damned much. He looked a lot more like he had before he'd become a parent. It was a reminder that once he had been something other than a father. He'd had big dreams, all of which had involved someone else.

At the bittersweet tug on his heart, he cleaned up his mess, satisfied that most of the glitter was gone, and went back into the room he was sharing with his daughter. She was flopped belly-down on one of the beds, her head bent over a thick book. One of the Percy Jackson series again, if Declan wasn't mistaken. The sight of her hit him in the chest with an overwhelming tidal wave of love. He absolutely adored his child and wouldn't wish her away. Not even for a chance at maybe a forever kind of love with the woman of his dreams. And who was to say that Livia was the woman of his dreams? What had he really known at eighteen? Not a whole hell of a lot.

"Hey." He waved to get Scarlett's attention. "Did you brush your teeth?"

With the aggravation that could only be expressed by a tween, she rolled her eyes. "Yes."

Then she fixed her gaze on his face and gestured to her own chin. "That's a big improvement."

"I know, I know. You hated that scraggly mess. I think the glitter stunt was just part of your evil plan."

She grinned and signed back, "I'll never tell."

Declan dove in, tickling her ribs until she shrieked with laugher and tapped out. Flopping across the end of her bed, he propped his head in his hand. "I do need you to promise me no glitter at your grandparents'. It's part of being a good guest."

"Of course not."

Satisfied with the promise, he rolled off the bed and headed for his own.

"Who's Livia?"

Was the Universe determined to keep throwing her in his face?

"Oh, you've picked up eavesdropping now? That's a habit I'd just as soon you not get from Ari."

Scarlett rolled her eyes again. "Come on, Dad."

He was Dad now, not Daddy. His heart squeezed a bit at this latest sign that she was growing up.

"Stop avoiding the question. Who is she?"

Declan knew his daughter. She'd never let this

go. It wasn't how she was wired. His kid was an absolute dog with a bone when she wanted to know something. It had led to more than one awkward conversation over the years as he'd done his best to handle her curiosity in a way that didn't punish her quest for information, even when it trod too close to the inappropriate.

"She's somebody I used to know a long time ago."

Scarlett crossed her hazel eyes and stuck out her tongue.

"Careful. It'll get stuck that way."

She blew a raspberry. "Sam said she was your old flame. Was she a girlfriend?"

Knowing he wouldn't get away with giving her nothing, he patted the bed next to him. She abandoned her own and flopped down beside him, invading his space like an overgrown puppy. He tangled their legs, engaging in their habitual foot wrestling as she settled in with her head at the opposite end where she could see him. He soaked in the closeness, not knowing how much longer she'd be willing to cuddle.

Settling back against the pillows, he lifted his hands and began the story-time routine they'd had since she was itty bitty, before she'd been fitted with hearing aids.

"So, a long time ago, before you were born, there was a stretch when your mom and I were broken up." And he'd meant for it to be forever. He'd been so over Bridget's bullshit at that point. "I was working out at the big apple orchard at the edge of town for the summer. It's where Abbey grew up."

"And Kyle?"

"And Kyle, before he came to live here with the rest of us and Gramma Joan."

Scarlett still hadn't quite gotten over being star struck by the fact that one of country music's great darlings was one of his foster brothers.

"Anyway, Abbey's cousin, Livia, was also in town for the summer to hang out with Abbey and help around the orchards, too."

"What was she like?"

This time, Declan didn't fight the pull of nostalgia as he thought back. "She was sweet, fun, funny. Smart as heck. She loved books, like you do. The first time I saw her, she was perched in the crook of an apple tree with a book in her lap, reading." He could still see her in those ridiculously short cutoffs that showed a mile of tanned legs, and that tight V-neck t-shirt. "She looked up and smiled at me, and my heart just fell—kerplunk—right at her feet and rolled over like a puppy waiting for a belly rub."

Scarlett giggled. "Love at first sight?" She was still at the age where she believed in such things.

"I thought so at the time."

"So what happened?"

"We spent most of the summer dancing around each other, becoming friends. I finally got up the nerve to kiss her at the top of the Ferris wheel on the Fourth of July at one of those little roadside carnivals." It still ranked as one of the best nights of his life.

"That was kind of it. There was no discussion. No stressing. No chase. We were just… together. She was from Mississippi and was planning on going to college in the fall at Ole Miss, and I was slated to be starting at UT. We were trying to decide how we were going to make long distance work, at least until one of us could transfer. Whatever we had to do to be together." And they'd made plans to level up their relationship, sealing their commitment with the ultimate intimacy.

"But you didn't."

For a moment, Declan floundered before he realized she was talking about college, not the night that had never happened. "No."

"What happened?"

He didn't want to relive this part of the story. It had sucked enough the first time.

Scarlett's face turned grim. "Mom happened. I happened."

Because he didn't want his child to take on blame for something that wasn't her fault, he didn't answer with a simple, "Yes."

"Your mom found out she was pregnant, and that was the end of that."

"Livia didn't want to see you anymore?" She sounded insulted on his behalf.

"I don't know. I never saw her again. I never even got a chance to talk to her."

Scarlett stared at him. "Why didn't you find her? Why didn't you tell her?"

Why indeed?

"I left to help your mom, and by the time I had an opportunity, Livia had already gone home, and too much time had passed."

"It's never too late to say you're sorry."

That had been a lesson he'd drilled into her, perhaps out of his own guilt. He felt a pinch at his own hypocrisy.

"I didn't know what to say." He'd never known what to say. And then he and Bridget had gotten married, and all his focus had been on trying to make that work.

"You should take advantage and talk to her now. They said she was in town."

Unwilling to commit and more than aware she'd probably call him a coward, Declan bent forward to ruffle Scarlett's hair.

"Daaaaad."

"We were just a sweet summer memory from a long time ago. She's long since moved on with her life."

Under other circumstances, he'd have busted his daughter for the level of side-eye she was shooting his way. Instead, he patently ignored it and scooted her off the bed. "C'mon. Time for bed. We've gotta get up early in the morning."

Scarlett crawled into the other bed, removing her hearing aids and settling under the covers. He turned out the light and settled back against his own pillows.

"What if she didn't move on with her life, Dad? Isn't it worth finding out?"

Knowing her hearing aids were out, he muttered the truth to himself. "Because I'm too afraid to ask the question."

* * *

TWO STEPS away from a food coma, Livia settled into one corner of the sectional sofa as Abbey maneuvered herself onto the chaise end. Kyle brought them both mugs of tea. "I'm gonna get out of y'all's way. If you need me, I'll be in the studio."

"Thanks." Abbey smiled and turned up her face for a kiss.

Then he was gone, and they were alone in their pajamas in the comfortable living room.

Abbey crossed her swollen ankles. "Okay, so how are things at home, really? You've been off the last several times we've talked. Are you and Jace struggling with the tree farm, having to deal with stuff without your parents?"

Livia wrapped both hands around her mug, absorbing the heat through her palms. "No. I meant what I said at dinner. Jace has everything running like clockwork. It's just hard having Mom and Dad gone, living it up on the road. And they should. They absolutely deserve the right to do that, especially after Daddy's heart attack. Jace is disgustingly happy with a sister-in-law that I adore, and she brought two new siblings into the family who are also a delight."

"That's how everybody else is doing. Not you."

Pregnancy had done nothing to dull Abbey's powers of observation.

"Work is… not great. I've been with the Wishful Public Library since I finished grad school. And I *loved* the job for a long time. But I told you about all the budget cuts. And then Autumn left to go write for a living. Which is great. I don't begrudge her following her passion at all. She's happy, and she totally deserves it after everything she and Judd went through. But I'm not nuts about the woman brought in to replace her. And my boss is still awful. I'm just… dissatisfied. And it feels like everybody is moving on with their life, except me. I never imagined that I was going to still be single at this stage in my life, and I'm lonely."

Abbey's brown eyes were soft with empathy and something else. "Is it possible that there's something more to that?"

Livia huffed a half laugh and sipped at her tea. "You mean other than the fact that I live in a town of five thousand people, and I've already gone out with, or am related to, all the single men in town?"

"I mean, there is an element of that," Abbey conceded. "I did live there for two years. But also, do you think you could have some unresolved feelings?"

"Unresolved feelings from what?"

"I saw your face when Granddaddy brought up Declan."

Livia couldn't fight the instinctive seizing in her chest. She breathed through it, working to keep her face neutral. "It just surprised me, is all. I really wasn't expecting it to come up. Certainly not in the present tense. I know you told me he does that—slips into the past—but I just didn't expect it. It's different seeing it than just hearing about it."

"You've never tried to contact him?"

Recognizing Abbey wouldn't be dissuaded, Livia focused on her mug. "No."

"Didn't you wonder all these years where he went? What happened?"

So many times. She shrugged. "Sure I did. But it doesn't matter, so why put myself through all the stress? You're besties with a bunch of his sisters, even during all those years you and Kyle weren't talking. You and I both know that if I really wanted to know, you could have asked. I'm sure they all know."

And she'd come so close to asking Abbey to do

exactly that. But she'd never been able to pull the trigger. Too afraid of what the answer might be. Not wanting to hear whatever excuse he cobbled together so many years after breaking her heart. He'd been important to her in so many ways, and she didn't want to find out that he hadn't really felt the same. She preferred to hang on to the bittersweet memories she had, rather than risk tainting them entirely with a truth she wasn't prepared to handle.

But she couldn't stop herself from asking now. "Do you know?"

"Yeah," Abbey admitted. "Part of it, anyway, though I didn't hear it from him directly. Do you want me to tell you?"

Livia couldn't read her expression, didn't know whether the reason was good or bad. So she shook her head. "It doesn't matter. At the end of the day, he ghosted me." And at least he'd done it before sleeping with her. She'd wanted him to be her first. If they'd crossed that bridge and then he'd disappeared, it would have been infinitely worse.

Concern and sympathy radiated off Abbey as she laid a hand on Livia's foot. "I know all these years we bonded over that because I felt like Kyle did the same thing to me. But it wasn't what I thought. And without getting into the specifics that aren't my story to tell, it's not what you thought with Declan, either. It wasn't because he wasn't interested or changed his mind about you."

Livia turned the idea of it over in her head. The longer she sat with it, the angrier she got. She'd imagined a million and one scenarios for why he'd left. None of the ones that hadn't been about her had involved him staying forever out of her life. "What good does it do to tell me that? If it wasn't about me, wasn't about him changing his mind, why did he never contact me? He's had twelve years."

Abbey pressed her lips together, clearly struggling not to spill whatever it was she knew. "Well, as I said, I don't know all the details. But it was complicated. And I think, in general, it's hard to come back after all that time, to admit you made a mistake."

"Was it a mistake?"

"I can't say for sure. I haven't talked to him directly myself. He avoids me when he comes home."

That got Livia's attention. "He's been home?" She hadn't realized he'd ever come back to Eden's Ridge.

"Yeah. He was in for one of his brothers' wedding this weekend."

This weekend. As in yesterday. Meaning… he might still be here.

For just an instant, she gave in to the longing. Because of course she did. Uncle Roy had opened this pandora's box, making her think all through dinner of the past and that summer when she'd fallen in love for the first time. This was the closest she and Declan had been since they were eighteen. He was prospectively mere miles away.

But she was no longer young and foolish. The hopeless romanticism she'd embraced for so long hadn't gotten her anywhere. She'd spent all these years looking for some romance novel hero who'd make her feel even a fraction of what she'd felt for Declan. Why the hell was she holding out for some perfect thing that couldn't possibly have been as good as she'd made it out to be in her memory?

As if reading her mind, Abbey said, "He's still here."

Livia slammed the door on all the what ifs and maybes that rose inside her. "Look, I love you. I'm glad that you and Kyle worked things out, and that everything that split you up in the first place wasn't what either of you thought it was. But that's not everybody. I know you just want me to be happy, but this is not the way to get me there.

Declan and I both moved on with our lives in completely separate places a long time ago. There is no point in walking down memory lane. I didn't come up here for this. I came to see you, to help with the Harvest Festival, and to get a little break from home." And, hopefully, to gain a little perspective.

Abbey finished her tea and set it aside. "I think you're wrong. But okay. I'll leave it alone."

"Thank you."

"Now help me up. I'm ready for bed, and I can't get off the sofa on my own."

CHAPTER 4

"You gonna give me the silent treatment the whole drive?"

Scarlett made a *hmph* and kept staring out the passenger side window.

"Family is important, kiddo. Your grandparents really want to spend some time with you so they can get to know you better." He bit his tongue before he could add, *even though your mom never has.*

That earned him a flat stare.

This visit had been on their schedule for a couple of months, but after all the time spent with her new favorite cousins, going to hang with Bridget's parents wasn't exactly at the top of her list. She'd met them before and had gotten on fine with them during the previous supervised visits, but this was the first full week that she'd ever spent with them, and her anxiety over it was manifesting in the form of a whole lot of tween attitude.

"Look, I know you're not excited. But think about it. They lost your mom, too. You're a piece of her. Arguably the very best piece, so give them a chance, okay? And if it's a disaster, I'm only a couple of hours away."

She folded her arms and blew out a slow breath. "Fine. I'll give it a chance. I'll do the thing. But you have to do something for me."

Declan hit her with a wary side eye. "What's that?"

"You have to go to the fair tonight."

He blinked at the unexpected request. "At the Harvest Festival?"

She nodded.

"Without you?"

"Yes."

"Why is that?"

"Because you need to have some fun."

Fun wasn't a part of his vocabulary beyond how it pertained to his kid. He was always too busy being the responsible dad. And while he wouldn't have been surprised that Scarlett thought he needed more fun in his life, he didn't think her request was quite that generic.

"Why do I get the feeling it's more than that?"

That earned him an eye roll. "Okay, fine. I heard through the family grapevine that Livia is going to be working the orchard's booth at the festival. You need to go talk to her."

Not letting on that his pulse had jumped at just the mention of her name, Declan played it cool. "What?"

"You heard me. You need to at least tell her what happened. If nothing happens after that, fine. Whatever. You've at least resolved the issue. But you never know. It might work out. You owe it to yourself to give this a try."

Resolve the issue? Who the hell had she been talking to? Had all the women in the family been meeting behind his back to have some kind of intervention?

"You think I have to try this?"

"I *know* you have to try this, Dad."

He wasn't sure how he felt about the idea of his kid playing matchmaker. That was *definitely* Ari's influence. She was a notorious romantic who claimed a significant role in the successful matchmaking of all of his sisters, and Declan had been warned that she was likely to set her sights on him if he stuck around long enough. Looked like that was accurate. But he'd been thinking about Livia for weeks now, considering what he'd do if he ran into her. Scarlett wasn't wrong. He'd come to the conclusion he needed resolution all on his own. Thanks very much. So, in the name of negotiation, he capitulated as he pulled into the driveway of a modest eighties-era two-story ranch. "Fine. I'll agree to go to the fair tonight and try to talk to her. But it means you have to give this visit with your grandparents a full twenty-four hours. Deal?"

She stuck out her hand to shake. "Deal."

Barbara and Ed Nicholson stepped out of the house, their faces bright with anticipation. The hands Barbara knit together gave away the nerves, as did the hold Ed had on her shoulder.

"Just remember, they're nervous, too," Declan told his daughter.

Scarlett sighed. "Right."

She might've dragged her feet a bit in getting out of the car. But she got out and strode up the walk with him.

"Hello, Scarlett!" There was a desperate edge to Barbara's enthusiastic greeting. At the sound of it, Scarlett eased closer to him.

Declan wrapped an arm around her shoulders. "Barbara, Ed, good to see you." Scarlett wasn't the only one who felt weird being here. These were his former in-laws. The people who'd raised the woman who'd walked away from her child without a backward glance. But Bridget had walked away from them, too, and he'd long ago recognized that the lack in his ex-wife hadn't come from her parents.

"Declan. Can we invite you in for a glass of tea?" Barbara asked.

He had less-than-zero desire for tea and pleasantries, but he'd do his due diligence to set his daughter at ease. "Sure. I'll just get Scarlett's bag first."

He retrieved her luggage and followed all of them inside.

Ed narrowed his eyes and stroked his chin. "You tryin' out a new fashion statement there, Declan? What's with the glitter?"

Lips pressed together, Declan shot Scarlett some side eye. Despite the trim, he *still* hadn't gotten all the glitter out. "That would be courtesy of your granddaughter here, who thought a glitter bomb was an appropriate send-off for Kendrick and Erin."

As they sat in the living room, Declan relayed the story, with interjections from Scarlett defending herself and Ari. By the end of it, they were all laughing.

The visit took longer than he wanted, but it was worth the delay to see Scarlett's shoulders relax. When they all rose to walk him out, she caught at his hand and began rapidly signing.

Don't forget what you promised. Talk to Livia. If you don't go, Ari will tell me.

With a bland stare, Declan signed back. *Keeping tabs on me?*

Scarlett matched his stare. "Duh."

He laughed and pulled her in for a big hug. "Love you, kid. I'll see you on Sunday."

"Bye, Daddy."

Declan held on to that *daddy* as he got back into the car and started the return trip to Eden's Ridge. He had two hours to figure out what the hell to say. Over the years, he'd ignored so many chances to go back and do the right thing by Livia, at least in terms of giving her an explanation for what happened. For all he knew, she'd somehow blamed herself for his defection, and that didn't sit well with him. He didn't know one way or the other. He'd avoided every opportunity to find out.

It was past time for him to man the hell up and go do the thing. He just hoped that Livia didn't spit in his face and that she'd give him a chance to explain.

And he hoped like hell he could get the last of the fucking glitter out of his beard before he went.

* * *

LIVIA HAD to admit that though Eden's Ridge was only half the size of Wishful—which was saying something about small—they knew how to put on a party. Several blocks of Main Street had been cordoned off for the celebration. Booths were set up from one end to the other, with artists, artisans, and food vendors galore. A stage was set up in the middle with a huge plywood sign announcing the lineup of musicians that would perform. Some bluegrass group had a re-spectable crowd gathered around the edges at the moment. Carnival rides had been erected in the long, narrow pasture behind the VFW a couple of streets off Main. People were everywhere, smil-ing, laughing, stuffing their faces with funnel cake and corn dogs and all the deep-fried good-ness that went along with a small town festival.

"I can't believe there's this kind of crowd on a Monday night." By this time on any given

Monday at home, Livia was already in sweat-pants, curled up with a book and a cup of tea.

"This is our biggest tourist week of the year," Aunt Faye explained. "Kicked off with the Harvest Festival this past weekend and stretches all the way through to next weekend for the Founder's Day celebration. The biggest crowds are on the weekends, of course, but we still have a lot of events and activities during the week for the locals."

The orchard booth had seen a steady stream of couples and families picking up apple butter, apple turnovers, and a multitude of other apple-themed wares. Livia had lost track of all the people she'd been introduced to. She appreciated the fact that not everyone knew her here like they did at home. Nobody had preconceived notions about who she was or what she wanted. The idea of that was far more appealing than she'd expected. She'd been considering some kind of change for a while now. Maybe that change could be here. She'd still be surrounded by family.

It's not family that has you thinking about Eden's Ridge.

The truth of it had her shifting uneasily behind the table. Her reasons for considering moving here were foolish in the extreme, because underneath it all was a hope that should've withered away years ago, based on the memory of a boy she couldn't forget. A boy who was now a man and no longer here.

You are an idiot.

"I'd say you three young'uns have earned a break," Uncle Roy announced. "Y'all go on now. We can handle the rest."

Abbey popped up from her seat with as much speed as her very pregnant belly would allow. "You don't have to tell me twice. I'm dying to walk around. C'mon, Livia. Let's go check out the fair."

"I would like to stretch my legs," she admitted.

Scooting out from behind the table, Kyle offered an arm to them both. "Ladies."

Livia waved him off. "There's not room for us to walk three across. Help your wife."

Abbey slid her arm through his, tipping her face up for a sweet kiss that had Livia sighing with just a little envy.

Someday.

The three of them entered the throngs of people. Livia hung back a little, following in their wake as they wandered through the stalls. For a while she stayed content browsing the available wares with an eye toward Christmas presents, but it didn't take long to feel like a third wheel. Abbey and Kyle couldn't help it. Everything they did called them out as a unit, and Livia wouldn't really have had it any other way. Abbey looked too happy, and she didn't begrudge her cousin for a moment.

She did wish she'd remembered a coat. The low seventies of the day had given way to temperatures plunging toward the forties now that the sun had gone down. The mountains were a lot colder than Mississippi at night. Shoving both hands into her jeans pockets, she hunched her shoulders and scanned a display of carved wooden bowls, wondering whether her mom might like one.

The warm weight of fabric draped over her shoulders.

"Oh, thanks, I—" She looked up, expecting to see that Kyle had unearthed a coat somewhere. But it wasn't her cousin-in-law.

Air clogged in her lungs.

He was broader than he had been at eighteen, his jaw more square beneath the close-cropped sandy beard. But she knew him. Knew the familiar hazel eyes and the slightly crooked grin. And just the sight of him had all that hope she'd tried to lock away, fighting to burst free.

"Declan. You're here." It was, perhaps, a foolish thing to say. But the moment had taken on the hazy quality of a dream or a spell, and she didn't quite trust her own eyes. Had she summoned him out of her own nostalgia?

"Better late than never."

That felt significant somehow. But before she could think why, their little bubble was broken.

"Ah, you made it. Great." Kyle stepped up, offering a hand and pulling Declan in for one of those back-thumping man hugs. "Good to see you, bro."

Declan nodded. "Back atcha. Abbey, you're looking well. I'm sorry we didn't manage to connect at the wedding last weekend."

Abbey sent him a speaking glance. "Well, you're here now. That's the important thing." She looped her arm back through Kyle's. "We're gonna let you two catch up."

Panic skittered through Livia. They couldn't just *leave* her here with him. But before she could get her brain back online to say so, they were gone, and she was on her own, save for the craftswoman watching from the back of the booth. Livia had no idea what to think or even what to say. What was the protocol when you came face to face with your first love? The one who'd walked away without a word?

Declan spoke first, hunching his shoulders a little as he shoved his hands into his own pockets in a gesture that screamed nerves. "Hey."

Somehow, knowing he was off-kilter too made her feel an iota calmer. "Hey."

His Adam's apple bobbed. "I can't begin to tell you how good it is to see you."

She found herself clutching at the lapels of the jacket he'd draped over her shoulders. If not for the feel of it wrapped around her, she might've reached out and tried to touch him, to verify he was flesh and blood and not a mirage. But the warmth of the leather was proof enough. Beneath the scent of old leather, she detected a hint of something that might've been cedar, and she had to resist the urge to turn her nose into the shoulder to take a better whiff.

Declan was staring at her, and she realized she had to actually respond. What had he said? That it was really good to see her. "Likewise. How have you been?" It was the most benign question she could manage under the circumstances.

He huffed a laugh. "I don't even know how to answer that." Darting a glance at the booth's attendant, he jerked his head. "Walk with me?"

What else could she say? "Okay."

She fell into step with him, aware of his proximity like a magnet to metal. Once he would've put his arm around her, and she'd have slid her hand into his back pocket. But they'd been separated by more than years and miles. She felt all of them as they made their way down the street, between stalls.

"Life is kind of in flux, at the moment," he admitted. "I've… been thinking about you. A lot."

"Really?" She knew she sounded skeptical. How could she not? If that were the case, why hadn't he said something, *done* something back when they still meant something to each other? She wasn't at all sure she wanted to hear the answer.

Declan dipped his head, staring at the ground for a long moment. "Listen, I… There are things I need to say."

Wary now, she glanced at him through lowered lashes. "About?"

He straightened, meeting her gaze head on. "You. Us. I handled things badly back when. As in… not at all. You deserved a lot better than that, and I just want you to know I'm sorry for hurting you."

Livia blinked, absorbing the statement. Much

as she'd wanted an apology all these years, she hadn't really expected to get one. And she didn't know what to do with this one. She fell back on manners. "I appreciate that."

He rocked back on his heels, shoving his hands back into his pockets, hesitating. "I'd… like to tell you what happened. If you're willing to listen."

For years she'd resisted the urge to chase down answers, terrified of what they might be. And here he was, offering them freely. Was the satisfaction of her curiosity worth the prospective pain?

"One ride on the Ferris wheel," he urged. "If you don't want to see me after that, I totally get it."

The Ferris wheel. Where they'd had their first kiss. Her pulse jumped. Was that significant? Or did he just want her as a captive audience for the duration of his tale?

The truth shall set you free. She didn't know if it would or not, but she couldn't pass up the opportunity to find out.

"Okay."

CHAPTER 5

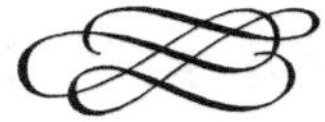

"Watch your hands." The attendant's voice was bored as he locked the safety bar across their laps.

Declan was very aware of Livia's hip and thigh pressed against his in the narrow seat. She was a bit curvier than she had been at eighteen, and the extra weight looked great on her. Her corn-silk blonde hair was still long and loose, as she'd worn it back then. His fingers itched to thread through it, but of course he did no such thing. He didn't drape his arm along the back of the gondola either. She wasn't his to touch anymore.

As the ride lurched into motion, moving them far enough that the next gondola could be loaded, her slim hands curled around the safety bar. Declan focused in on the neat ovals of her nails, painted a blush pink. He remembered the feel of those nails scraping against his scalp during lazy summer evenings sprawled on a picnic blanket by the pond at the orchard. She'd been able to make him purr.

"So…" Livia drawled the word in an awkward prompt.

The sound reminded Declan that he only had the length of this ride to say his piece. Despite how much he'd thought about this moment, considered what to say and how to say it, he still didn't really know where to begin. It was why he'd never done this. He'd never known how to face her. How to admit to his own mistakes. But he'd made Scarlett a promise, and, more to the point, he'd promised himself. He set his own hands on the safety bar to keep from trying to reach for her.

"That summer I spent with you was the best one of my life." Beginning with the absolute truth seemed a reasonable tactic. "When we talked about school, about our plans after, I was fully invested. I had every intention of following through. On that. On the… other things we had planned."

He'd planned to romance her. To make their

first time something she'd remember for the rest of their lives. He'd pulled every string he had, called in every favor to get the cabin up at Watauga Lake. And it had all been for naught.

"The day I was supposed to pick you up to go to the lake, you were all I was thinking about. Hell, you were all I was thinking about all summer, from the moment I saw you up in that tree. And then—" He broke off on a sigh and looked over at her. "You remember me telling you about my high school girlfriend, Bridget?"

Livia's gray eyes narrowed, her mouth tipping down in a very reserved sort of frown. "Yes."

"She showed up at the house. I guess maybe I should've expected something. She'd been calling off and on for a month. I'd just ignored it. We weren't together anymore, and I didn't want to talk to her. Her family had moved from Eden's Ridge right after graduation. It was why I'd broken up with her then. The timing just made sense. She was finally leaving, and I figured it would be simple and easy. But it wasn't simple." Declan took another breath and admitted what he hadn't been able to say back then. "She was pregnant."

Pressed against her as he was, he felt Livia's jerk of surprise. "Oh."

"Yeah." Uncomfortable, he rubbed at the back of his neck. "She was understandably freaked out. We had a lot of complicated shit to sort through, and after that bomb was dropped, I didn't know how to face you. I didn't know how to tell you that everything we'd planned had just gotten massively derailed by something entirely outside of our control."

"You have a child." Her tone was one of numb disbelief. He couldn't blame her. It had been a hell of a shock to him.

"A daughter. Scarlett. She's the light of my life."

"You married her mother." It wasn't a question.

That Livia instantly knew that, even after all these years, meant something to him. With his background and all the struggle he and his own single teenaged mom had endured before he'd ended up in the foster system, he wasn't capable of making any other decision when it came to his own child.

"Yeah. We tried to make it work. But, I mean, we were eighteen. It was a major struggle. We'd split for a reason, and the financial burden, when neither of us had more than a high school educa-tion, was rough. Bridget was so angry and resentful. She'd had big plans and none of them had included a kid. When Scarlett was born, it just got worse. She was born with profound hearing loss, which presented a whole new boatload of challenges. Ultimately, Bridget bailed on us when Scarlett was three." And hard as it had been to do things on his own, it was easier than dealing with his ex-wife's mercurial moods and tantrums.

Livia's hands tightened on the railing until the knuckles turned white, but her voice was mild. "Some women aren't meant to be mothers."

"No," he agreed. "I thought about you after my divorce, but I figured you'd moved on and wouldn't want to hear from me, and I was busy trying to keep our heads above water, so I didn't do anything about it. The fact is, I've had so many opportunities over the years when I thought about you and wondered where you were and how you were doing. My sisters stayed friends with Abbey. I could've found out. Gotten your number or email address. I always wanted to come clean, but I never knew how."

She stayed quiet for a full revolution of the Ferris wheel, looking out over the bright lights of rides and the throngs of people far below, but Declan didn't think she really saw the view. "Why now?"

"Honestly? Other than the fact that I'm still thinking about you, my niece and daughter shanghaied me into it. Given some of what Scarlett said, I suspect there was a family meeting and intervention planned if I hadn't showed up tonight. But I'd already decided to track you down. Once I found out you'd be here, it was just a matter of working up the nerve."

He could tell she was still processing everything he'd said as they made another circuit of the wheel. She'd always been a careful thinker. He only wished he had a better read on what those thoughts were.

"Anyway, that's the story. That's why I bailed. Why I walked away without a word. And I'm so damned sorry I was a coward. I know hurt you, and that was never my intention. Life just got away from me."

When she said nothing by the time they reached the bottom again, and the attendant unlocked the safety bar, Declan figured that was it. She was done with him. At least he'd gotten to say his piece.

He slipped out of the gondola and turned back, automatically offering his hand to help her out.

She took it, curling those long, slim fingers

around his and stepping out herself. But she didn't let go immediately, and his heart gave a thump of unwilling hope.

"Where's your daughter now?"

"Visiting with her maternal grandparents for the week. It's just me."

Livia hesitated, gaze searching his face for a long moment. "Do you maybe want to take in the fair together?"

Declan's smile spread huge and wide because this was a second chance he hadn't expected.

"I'd love to."

* * *

OF ALL THE reasons Livia had imagined over the years for why Declan had disappeared, his high school girlfriend being pregnant hadn't been one of them. He'd been so over Bridget that summer. But of course he'd done what he'd perceived as the right thing when she'd turned up pregnant. Livia had no idea how she'd have reacted to the news at eighteen. Would it have broken her heart any less knowing he'd married someone else out of duty? Probably not, but it would've been a reason. One that definitely had nothing to do with her. He hadn't changed his mind about her.

About them. Circumstances had changed it for him.

The knowledge of that was worth something. As was the fact that he was here, all these years later, a single dad. One who'd apparently thought of her over the years as much as she'd thought of him.

He wasn't the same. How could he be after everything he'd been through, all the struggles he'd endured, raising a child on his own? And a special needs child at that. But Livia could still see shades of the boy she'd loved as they strolled through the fair, each of them nibbling on a corn dog. Now that the biggest mystery had been solved, she wanted to know everything. It was as if, once she gave in to curiosity, it was running wild.

"So, what are you doing now? Where do you even live?"

"Well, that's changing, actually. We've been near Nashville for most of the last ten years. But we're moving back to Eden's Ridge. I just took a job managing the Eden's Ridge Artisan Guild and Education Center. It was time to come home. I wanted Scarlett to be around more stable female influences as she gets older, and being close to my sisters accomplishes that."

He'd been close to his myriad of foster siblings back in the day, and Livia was glad he still had those family connections. Not wanting to leave family was a big part of why she'd never considered moving away from Wishful before. Starting over completely on her own somewhere was overwhelming, to say the least.

Lost in thought, Livia almost plowed into a gaggle of teenage girls gathered around the high striker, but Declan snagged her by the elbow, neatly tugging her out of the way. "What about you?"

The teenage boy with the giant mallet swung, and the puck went rocketing three-quarters of the way up the column, to the cheers of his fan club.

Turning away, Livia continued down the midway, half tempted to clutch at her elbow to hold in the tingle of his touch. "I'm a children's librarian."

Declan grinned. "I always knew you'd do something with books. Still living in Wishful?"

"Yes. Though I'm starting to wonder if that's where I need to be." She hadn't meant to say it, but the words just slipped out. Probably because the whole thing had been on her mind since she'd arrived in Tennessee.

"Why's that?"

She'd opened this can of worms, and maybe it would be good to discuss it with someone who wasn't family. "Everything's changing. Or it is for everyone else. Seems like everybody I know is moving on with the next phase of their life. My baby brother got married. My parents have turned over the running of the farm to us and are seeing the country by RV in their retirement. But Jace has a degree in forestry, so he doesn't really need me. My boss at the library is a heinous hell beast. I've just been… not exactly unhappy, but not content either. I'm restless, and I don't quite know what to do about it."

"What would you rather do instead?"

"I don't know. I love being a librarian. I've never thought of being anything else. You know how much I love books. I love being involved in the community, and I love kids. I totally expected to have some by now." Embarrassed by the admission, she bit into her corn dog to keep herself from talking more.

"So, there's nobody special for you back home?" His gaze dropped to her left hand where it gripped the corn dog stick, and she felt the weight of it.

"No one who's mattered." She couldn't stop

herself from looking up at him. Because he had mattered. More than she'd let herself believe.

Needing to shake off the seriousness of the conversation, she shrugged. "I really don't know what I want to do. I've only recently begun to legitimately consider doing something else or going somewhere else. And of course, that's going to depend on being able to find gainful employment. Because being able to pay one's bills is a thing."

"True story."

They finished their corn dogs and disposed of the sticks and napkins in a nearby trash can.

"Step right up, folks! Try your skill at busting balloons!"

Livia glanced over at the stall where an array of colorful balloons were tacked to a plywood backing. A veritable ocean of stuffed animal prizes hung around it, including a massive elephant in eye-popping pink. It reminded her of another prize from another fair from years ago. She still had that thing tucked in the back of her closet, one of the best memories of that summer.

The carny manning the game noticed her attention. "A pretty prize for a pretty lady. Sir, how's your dart game?"

Declan stepped up to the counter and began fishing tickets out of his pocket.

"Oh, that's really not necessary," Livia began.

With mock severity, he glared at her. "I am duty bound to win you a stuffed animal. It's part of guy code."

That implied that this chance encounter was a date. More excited by the prospect of that than she cared to admit, Livia stepped up beside him. "Fair enough. Let's see how you do."

Declan accepted the three darts, testing the weight of them in his hand. He eyed the board at the back, clearly trying to gauge the distance. Rolling on the balls of his feet, he tossed the first dart. It took a nosedive and thunked off the bottom third of the board without sticking.

"Two to go!"

"That was a practice shot," Declan announced.

Eyes narrowed, he threw the second dart. This one hit higher and actually stuck in the target, but it didn't hit any of the balloons.

He glared down at the last dart in his hand. "Are these defective?"

Livia pressed her lips together to keep from laughing.

Declan tossed the final dart, which glanced off one of the balloons, but didn't break it. He set his hands on his hips. "I was better at this twelve years ago."

So he remembered.

"Tough luck, son. Would you like to try again?"

"Actually, I'd like to try." Livia dug out some of her own tickets and handed them over to the attendant.

"Sure thing, little lady." The guy handed her three darts.

She rolled them between her fingers, testing the points. They were a little dull, but not terrible. Taking position, she fixed her gaze on an orange balloon in the top left quadrant and let the dart fly.

Pop!

A little cheer went up around her from other waiting patrons, but she ignored everyone, taking aim at a blue balloon in the top right quarter. Toss. *Pop!*

She didn't stop to look at anyone before lining up her final shot with a red balloon in the dead center. On an exhale she released, watching as the dart flew through the air to bury itself in the board, popping her third balloon.

The carny looked equal parts impressed and annoyed. "Nice job. Your choice of prizes."

"The elephant."

He used a hook and retrieved the stuffed animal from where it hung and handed it over. Only then did she turn toward Declan.

His smile was rueful. "I feel like my masculinity is being impugned."

Livia smiled sweetly. "Did I mention my brother and I have been playing darts for the last twenty years to decide who gets what chores around the farm?"

"You did not." He raised his hands in a slow clap. "I know when I'm bested. Bravo."

She handed the elephant over with a grin. "Why don't you take it home to Scarlett? Unless you'd like to keep her yourself to remember tonight by?"

Declan hooked an arm around the elephant and took Livia's free hand, tugging her a step closer. "I'm not going to need anything to remember every moment of tonight."

Her pulse leapt, and she curled her fingers around his. "Neither will I."

CHAPTER 6

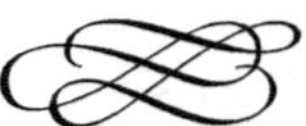

The crowds had thinned considerably. All around them, food vendors were shutting down for the night. Many of the artisans had likewise shuttered their booths. The whole place would close soon. Declan wasn't ready for the night to end.

Apparently Livia wasn't either. Fingers still tangled with his, she turned toward him. "One last ride on the Ferris wheel before we call it a night?"

"Absolutely."

They stowed the elephant with the attendant and settled into their gondola. This time, he put his arm around her. She snuggled in, a sign of ease and trust he wasn't sure he deserved but wasn't about to waste. It felt too good to hold her, to look up into the cloudless sky and marvel at the ocean of stars that blanketed the little town that was the only place that had ever been home.

Could it be home for Livia? What were the chances that they'd both be looking for a change at the same time? She'd seemed almost embarrassed by not having her life entirely figured out. He had plenty of practice with that state of affairs. If he'd known what the hell he was doing for more than five minutes at a time at any point in the last twelve years, he'd called it good. Tonight was no exception. The past hours with her had been a gift that left him greedy for more. More conversation. More touches. More long looks. Simply more of her. He'd always wanted more of her.

As they stopped at the very top for passengers below to disembark, Declan shifted a little to face her. Livia lifted her head, meeting his gaze. He couldn't stop himself from stroking his fingers across her cheek to tuck a strand of hair behind her ear, letting his fingers linger.

"Tonight's been awesome. Getting to reconnect and clear the air."

The corners of her mouth tipped up into the faintest of smiles. "Yeah."

Once, he'd have simply leaned in to taste that smile. But he was a lot more cautious than he was at eighteen, and he didn't want to risk screwing this up again. "I'd really like to kiss you."

Those lips bowed further, her eyes going dark. "I really wish you would."

There is a God.

She met him halfway, tipping her face up to his. They both sighed at the contact, melting into each other. And oh God, it was better than he remembered. Her kiss was at once familiar and foreign, marrying the boy he'd been with the man he was. His blood popped and fizzed like champagne, the taste of her leaving him dizzy and struggling not to dive too deep, too fast. With every second that rolled by, it seemed the stress and strain of years fell away, until the only thing remaining was her.

A throat cleared from somewhere close by.

Declan broke the kiss, realizing they were back at the bottom and the attendant was waiting for them to get off the ride. He tightened his arm around Livia as he pressed his brow to hers for just a few more seconds, wishing they had more time.

"Sorry, man, we're shutting down for the night."

He untangled himself and flashed an apologetic smile at the guy. "Sorry."

They waited until the lap bar was unlocked, and Declan scrambled out, reaching back to help Livia onto the platform. She scooped up the elephant and thanked the attendant. In the time it had taken them to finish their ride, it seemed most of the rest of the fair had packed up.

"Looks like we're more or less closing the place down."

She glanced around as if noticing for the first time that most of the crowd had disappeared. "I'm guessing Abbey and Kyle headed home a while ago."

Declan sent up a quick prayer of thanks. He'd get a little longer with her, after all. "I'll drive you back."

Hand in hand, they made their way down the quiet streets to where he'd parked his car. Neither of them spoke much, and he appreciated the fact that being silent with her was just as easy as talking. Everything with Livia had always been easy and comfortable. He'd taken it for granted at eighteen. He didn't want to do that again.

"How much longer are you here?"

"Two weeks. I cashed in a huge chunk of vacation days. After that, I've gotta get back to work.

And our busy season is about to start at the farm. We've got a lot of prep to do before Thanksgiving. Jace has most of it under control, but it's all hands on deck for the holidays."

She'd always taken family obligations seriously. It was one of the things he liked about her. He felt exactly the same about his extended foster family, so he understood that considering a life somewhere other than Wishful was a huge deal for her. But he couldn't stop thinking about how, if he could convince her to move to Eden's Ridge, they could have the second chance they never really got all those years ago. He wanted that almost more than his next breath. But he recognized that now wasn't the time for a blatant, full-court press, so he'd have to settle for whatever additional time he could get with her. And he intended to wrangle as much of the next two weeks as possible.

* * *

THE SENSIBLE SEDAN was a far cry from the ancient pickup Declan had driven back in the day, but he still held Livia's hand across the center console on the drive back to the orchard. The hum of awareness shivered around them, as if they stood on a precipice. Livia had a general sense of the fragility of whatever lay between them just now. They were both more cautious, so very aware of how life could intervene at any moment. This wasn't an uncomplicated summer, where possibilities spun out in an endless array of wonder. They both had responsibilities. Lives that didn't mesh.

And still, the curve of his fingers around hers gave birth to an irrational, impossible hope. The *what if?* she hadn't allowed herself to consider before. It was a dangerous and potentially painful question, and a part of Livia wanted to be a reckless optimist. To believe that he was the answer to the wish she'd made back home. But she wasn't the starry-eyed teen she'd been. And he had more than himself to consider.

Declan pulled up to the house and shut off the car. Kyle and Abbey had left the porch light on for her. They both slid out and made their way up the couple of steps to the front door.

"Do you suppose Abbey's on the other side waiting to blink the porch light if we take too long, the way your Aunt Faye used to do?"

"If her claims about me being her favorite cousin are true, then no."

Declan stepped closer, sliding his hands

around her waist. "You're my favorite of her cousins."

Smirking, Livia slid her arms around his neck. "Met a lot of us, have you?"

"Nope, but you'd win, anyway. Hands down."

One moment, they were grinning at each other. The next, they were kissing again. Her whole body sighed in pleasure, relaxing against him. The Ferris wheel kiss had been sweet, a tentative exploration. This was more. Declan's arms tightened beneath the jacket she still wore, hauling her closer, up to her toes to take her mouth in a bid to show her he wasn't the tentative boy he'd been. Pressed up against the heat of him, it was more than obvious that the man still wanted her. The idea of it was a heady drug, one that threatened to overcome her good sense.

Again, he was the one who pulled back, clear reluctance in the motion as he settled his brow against hers with a little laugh. "How can this feel like yesterday?"

Not immune, Livia combed her fingers through his hair in the way she knew he'd always liked, relishing the little purr he made. "Nostalgia is a powerful thing."

He straightened enough to peer down at her. "You think that's all this is?"

She swallowed, aware that her answer mattered. "No. No, I don't."

"Good." Gently releasing her, he stepped back, putting space between them. "I'll see you tomorrow, Livia."

More than a little giddy at the prospect, she slid off the jacket, handing it back to him. "Tomorrow."

She waited on the porch until he'd gotten in the car, and he sat there waiting for her to go inside. They were both grinning again when she broke the stalemate with a wave and backed through the front door. She shut it and collapsed back against the wood panels with a gusty sigh, half tempted to keep going and melt into a puddle on the floor, because this was Declan. He was *here.* He was moving back. And that opened the door for possibilities she hadn't even considered.

A light went on in the living room.

Livia muffled a shriek before she spotted Abbey perched in the big armchair, hands folded over her enormous pregnant belly, her tongue tucked firmly in cheek. "Looks like someone had a good night."

Shoving away from the door, Livia strode into the living room, grabbing a pillow off the sofa and hugging it to her chest before falling face first onto the cushions with another happy sigh. "Yes. Yes, I did. Thank you for your interference, Miss Nosy."

"I really didn't do anything. Kyle just made sure it was widely known in the family that you were going to be here. What Declan did with that was up to him. I gather you finally talked?"

"Yeah. Thanks. You already knew about his daughter, didn't you?"

Abbey nodded. "I heard a few years ago. You were so insistent on not wanting to know anything about him, I kept the lid on it. But I wouldn't have pushed you back toward him if I didn't think there was something still there. Was I right?"

"You weren't peeking out the sidelight?"

Abbey lifted her nose with an imperious expression. "I have more restraint than that."

"Restraint or an inability to move fast because of Hank the Tank?" She eyed her cousin's massive belly.

"The two are not mutually exclusive. So? Dish! You spent all night with him. That's good, right?"

"Yeah, our attraction is still alive and well." Livia tucked the pillow beneath her head. "He's moving back here."

"Really? I didn't know that. Does it change things for you?"

"I don't know. One night hardly seems enough justification to make any major decisions over." And if she kept telling herself that, she might not make a foolish mistake.

"You're here for two weeks."

"I came for you."

"Psh. If you think I'm going to begrudge you the chance to rekindle things with Declan, you don't know me as well as I thought you did. You and I are fine. Besides, I have a vested interest in this. If he is moving back here and you fall for him all over again, maybe it'll convince you to move up here."

Livia shot her the side eye.

"Oh, don't act like you weren't thinking about it, anyway. How awesome would it be to come back to be with him?"

A wish come true. But she was no Cinderella.

"Attraction doesn't pay the bills. Wherever I might prospectively go, I need a job. Preferably one I'd actually like. Eden's Ridge doesn't seem to be just overflowing with opportunities for a librarian."

"You don't know that. You haven't looked yet."

"I can't imagine that a library in a town even

smaller than Wishful has a budget any better off than ours."

"You never know. The library here serves all of Stone County. It's worth checking."

"And I probably will check. But I'm not moving here just for Declan. Things are too up in the air. I can't turn my life upside down on a maybe. I need more certainty than that." But she couldn't deny that she was tempted.

"Baby, there are no guarantees in life other than death and taxes. If there's more than an iota of a shot for you and Declan, isn't it worth taking it?"

That was the sixty-four-thousand-dollar question. One she wouldn't allow herself to consider. Not yet.

"I'll take the next couple of weeks and whatever they bring and be grateful for finally getting closure. It's more than I expected to have with him."

Abbey made a noise of disgust. "Closure? Really? That's *all* you're willing to reach for?"

"It's the only thing I'm guaranteed now." Hell, he'd said he'd see her tomorrow, but they hadn't actually made plans, and he didn't even ask for her number. The realization brought her back down to earth. "I've got enough uncertainty in my life without adding the complication of Declan to it."

Catching the twist of Abbey's expression, Livia just raised a brow. "Careful, or your face will get stuck like that."

"I'm biting my tongue so hard right now. It's your life, your heart, so it's your call. I know that. Just… promise me you'll give him a chance while you're here. See what comes of it."

"It might be nothing."

"Or it might be everything."

Livia's heart gave a little bump. "Fine. I promise to give him the two weeks."

"Fair enough. We should get to bed. You need your beauty sleep." Abbey scooted to the edge of the chair and held out her hands. "Now help me up. I'm stuck!"

CHAPTER 7

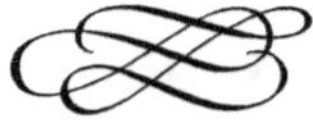

After dropping Livia at the orchard, Declan was way too amped to go back to the inn and straight to bed. He ought to be figuring out his plan for how to tackle all the tasks necessary for the upcoming move. Instead, he found himself reliving that last kiss as he drove aimlessly toward town.

The one on the Ferris wheel had been innocent. Sweet, even. A reminder of who they'd once been to each other. The one on the porch… That had been a kiss between a man and a woman who wanted each other. Who had life experience enough to know what that entailed and were all in. For a fleeting moment, he wondered what might have happened if either of them had their own place or some anonymous hotel room instead of nosy family who could interrupt at inopportune moments. Would they have ended up in bed, naked and tangled, racing toward the conclusion that had seemed inevitable at eighteen? Or would one of them have come to their senses and stopped the runaway train of lust on top of nostalgia?

Probably best they hadn't had the opportunity to find out.

Finding himself on one of the side streets of downtown that hadn't been blocked off for the festival, he glanced up to see a light still on in Mick's apartment above Webster's Hardware. His brother had always been a night owl. Before he could think better of it, Declan eased into a parking spot at the curb and headed up.

The door swung open almost immediately after his knock, revealing a woman and a dog inside Mick's place. At least, he was pretty sure the rotund, furry thing that resembled a gray and brown potato with legs was a dog. He couldn't be sure.

"Oh, I'm sorry. I didn't mean to interrupt. I didn't realize you had company."

"No, no, it's fine. This is my neighbor, Juliette

Chen, and her dog Derp. Juliette, my brother Declan."

She offered a tired smile. "Nice to meet you."

Declan nodded a hello. Given the squished face, slightly bulging eyes, and tongue that seemed to just hang out the left side of the dog's mouth, Derp was aptly named.

"She had to work late," Mick continued, "so I was taking care of the little guy for her."

Juliette scooped up her rotund pooch. "You're a godsend, Mick. A really great friend."

Declan noted the subtle flinch from his brother at the "friend" comment. That told him everything he needed to know about this situation.

He stepped back as she moved toward the door with her happily panting furry companion. With another nod of acknowledgment, she crossed the hall and went into the apartment on the other side. As the door shut behind her, Declan fixed Mick with a look.

Mick's dark brows drew together. "What?"

"Now it begins to make sense."

"What are you talking about?"

"You feeling the singledom. How long has she shunted you into the friend zone?"

"I don't know what you're talking about."

He stepped fully into the apartment. "Really? You're gonna go with that?"

Hand still on the door, Mick offered a bland stare. "Did you just come to bust my chops for random reasons, or did you have a reason for showing up?"

"I saw Livia tonight."

His brother's whole demeanor changed, the attitude melting away into a combination of interest and concern. "Oh. Do we need a beer for this conversation?"

"I wouldn't say no."

Mick retrieved a couple of Yeunglings, and they sprawled on opposite ends of the big faux-leather sofa.

"So? What happened?"

"Kyle made sure I knew she'd be at the festival tonight."

"Brother, we *all* knew that. We were ready to press-gang you into attendance if you hadn't acted on your own."

Declan paused, the bottle halfway to his lips. "Nice to know where everyone's loyalties lie. Anyway, we talked. I made my apology and explained what happened all those years ago."

When he didn't immediately continue, Mick

growled. "You're burying the lead. How did she take all that?"

"You're getting as bad as Ari."

"She's rubbing off on all of us. Quit stalling."

"It went… so much better than I thought it would. We ended up hanging out all night, talking, catching up, riding rides. It was very date-like. And it was just like… I'd seen her yesterday. All the old feelings are still there."

Mick whooped. "I *knew it!*"

Declan had to fight back his grin because his own enthusiasm was bubbling just beneath the surface. "I don't know how much of it is nostalgia and chemistry and how much is something more, but she's here for two weeks, so it seems like I'll get the chance to find out."

"That's awesome, man. I'm happy for you. When do you see her again?"

He opened his mouth to answer and realized that, after that mind-blowing kiss on the porch, they hadn't actually made plans. But he'd said tomorrow because he couldn't imagine waiting more than overnight. And because it was what he'd said every day during their summer together.

"I'll head back out to the orchard in the morning." If she was tied up, he could be a grownup and get her number and make proper plans.

"All of this sounds awesome. So why are you here? Because I know you, bro. You wouldn't just show up to rehash your night, complete with googly eyes. Something's stuck in your craw about this, so what is it that's bothering you?"

Was that why he'd come here? Because he needed to talk it out? Figure out what was circling around in the back of his brain now that it wasn't clouded by feelings?

"Well, her life isn't here, for one. I'm in flux and getting ready to move here from Nashville in a matter of weeks. Add to that, I'm a single parent. I don't have the luxury of jumping heart first and risk falling flat on my face." No matter how much he wanted to. "I've got more than me to worry about."

And so his feet came firmly back down to earth as his adult brain began throwing up all the potential problems of getting involved with Livia again.

"Man, I respect and give you mad props for all your focus on Scarlett. You're a good dad. But how often have you used your kid as an excuse not to make a move or to take a step or to not do the scary thing?"

The instant clench of discomfort told Declan there was truth to the statement. "Even if that is a little bit true, Livia is different."

"Sure, she's different. The way you've always talked about her is like she was The One. She's certainly the one who got away. So what are you gonna do to make sure she doesn't do that again?"

Hold on and don't let go.

Ignoring the instant answer that bloomed in his brain, he shrugged. "I don't know. I have eleven thousand other things I need to deal with this week." A faint flicker of guilt over the lack of organization around that had him tipping back the beer for another sip.

"Well, you have a week without your kid. And, yeah, you have a lot of shit you need to take care of to get ready for the move. But when are you going to get this shot again? The woman you loved, that you have secretly pined over for more than a decade, is back in your life, willing to give you another shot. That says to me she's got a lot of those old feelings, too. Which maybe means those feelings were very real on both sides. If I were you, I'd be coming up with every excuse under the sun to spend more time with her. See if this is just nostalgia and chemistry or if there's a potential for something real. And if there is? Don't let her go again, man."

Every cell in his body agreed with Mick. He wanted to jump all in. But he'd learned caution since he'd last done that. If he leapt again, he needed to know she'd be there to catch him.

"For now, I'm just gonna start with breakfast."

* * *

LIVIA WOKE SLOWLY, her lips still tingling from Declan's kiss, her body loose and languid and aroused. Her hand stretched out, reaching for him, wanting to cuddle into his warmth and make lazy love to start the day. When she found nothing but an empty stretch of sheets, she came fully alert, disappointment crashing through the remaining haze of the dream. He wasn't here. Just like he hadn't been there twelve years ago for the romantic weekend they'd planned to take their relationship to the next level.

Before she could fall down the rabbit hole of negativity, she scrubbed both hands over her face. Of course he wasn't here. She hadn't invited him up. Wouldn't have, as this was her cousin's house. God, how would *that* have gone, if she'd pulled him inside and Abbey had still been sitting in the living room waiting? Abbey probably would've cheered them on. How awkward would *that* have been? Even if she'd stayed quiet and they'd never known she was there, Livia didn't think she'd have been able to relax enough for any kind of intimacy, knowing Abbey and Kyle were just down the hall.

Getting ahead of yourself, girl.

A couple of truly delicious kisses did not automatically mean they ought to fall into bed. That was just her long-denied libido talking. She'd trusted him enough to be willing to go there once, and life had intervened. After last night, now she understood he'd had reasons. Good ones. But she hadn't forgotten how it had felt watching day bleed into night, waiting, waiting, waiting, and Declan never showing. Never even sending word that he couldn't make it.

He'd well and truly broken her heart, and she'd never really gotten over it. That same heart wanted to believe in him now. To throw her immediately back in the deep end so they could pick back up where they'd left off. But his life was complicated, and her brain was going to take longer to get onboard. Yeah, he'd said he wanted to see her again, but he hadn't firmed up any plans for when or what. She refused to spend her time here waiting around on Declan Callahan like the lovesick teenager she'd once been.

A long, hot shower improved her disposition considerably. Knowing coffee would take care of the rest, she dressed and headed downstairs in search of some. She found Abbey and Kyle in the kitchen, tucked up beside each other in the window seat, looking like a romance novel happily ever after. Feeling like an intruder on what looked like an intimate moment, she hesitated at the threshold, wondering if she should turn around.

Abbey glanced up. "Good morning! We've got breakfast at the big house this morning. Mama said she'd making pancakes."

Kyle rubbed the mound of her belly. "This one can't get enough of those."

"It's the bacon," his wife pronounced. "See?" She pointed to where her belly vibrated with a thump. "He kicks for bacon. Let's go."

Knowing there would absolutely be coffee at the farmhouse, Livia waited as Kyle hefted Abbey to her feet, and they all fell into step for the short walk. The sun hung just over the horizon, washing the sky beyond the orchard in a watercolor splendor that suggested they were in for a beautiful day.

"How did you sleep?" Abbey's grin suggested she knew Livia had been treated to more than PG dreams.

"Fine."

Livia definitely didn't want to talk about her dreams. She still didn't know what to do with the fact that thoughts of Declan brought as much pain as excitement. She'd learned better than to let herself give in to anticipation. Hope was a dangerous thing. It bred expectations, and expectations led to more disappointment. Better to assume last night was all she was going to get.

Already depressed by the idea of it, Livia hung back as they all trooped into the house and headed for the kitchen, where she could hear the murmur of voices and smell the delicious aroma of coffee.

Aunt Faye turned from the stove, where a small mountain of pancakes already sat on a tray by her elbow. "Good morning, y'all. We've got company for breakfast."

Company?

Livia's gaze shot to the table. And there, sitting beside Uncle Roy with a mug in his hands, exactly as he had so many times before, was Declan.

"You're here." It was exactly what she'd said at

the fair last night, but there was that same sense of unreality at seeing him.

One corner of his mouth quirked up in a self-deprecatory smile. "Mornin'. I forgot to get your number last night."

Uncle Roy huffed in satisfaction. "Told you he was sweet on you."

If Declan was embarrassed by being called out, he didn't show it. "I figured I'd take a shot that y'all were all still early risers and come on over."

"Of course. You're always welcome," Aunt Faye insisted. "We love getting visits from our people."

Something flickered over Declan's face at the reference to him as one of "our people," and it occurred to Livia that it had been a brave thing for him to tromp over here like this without knowing how the family would react. So far as she knew, he hadn't seen or spoken to any of them in twelve years, either. Then again, as locals, they'd all probably known some version of the truth she'd so staunchly avoided all this time.

She was still staring at him, unable to get her brain to kick into gear, when he rose from his seat and crossed to the coffeemaker. He opened a cabinet and pulled down a mug, pouring a cup and adding one sugar and a healthy splash of half and half from the fridge before giving it a stir and bringing it over to her.

"I figure you still need some of your favorite go-go juice to get rolling in the morning."

Stunned, she accepted the mug and sipped. "You remember how I take my coffee?"

"I haven't forgotten a thing about you." The low murmur slid over her like a caress.

Livia wanted to pull him in and claim another kiss as a start to her day. The punch of it would probably be far more effective and a lot quicker than the caffeine. But she still felt awkward about this around her family, so she held herself back, lifting the mug in a toast instead. "Thank you."

"I didn't know what your plans were for the day, so I thought I'd swing by early to put in my bid if you had any free time."

He'd promised her tomorrow and here he was, exactly as he'd said he would be. Her romantic heart sent up a cheer. *See? He's still that guy we loved. Everything from before was just a misunderstanding.*

"I don't actually know what I'm supposed to be doing today. Part of why I'm here is to help with the Harvest Festival."

Aunt Faye turned from the stove, gesturing

with the spatula. "Oh honey, no. That was just a thinly veiled excuse to get you up here for a longer visit. You two go, have fun. Enjoy yourselves."

Well, obviously, they were on board with the rekindling of this flame. Livia wasn't sure how she felt about that, but she wasn't about to look the gift of more time with him in the mouth. With a wry smile of her own, she met his hazel gaze. "It seems I'm at loose ends."

Declan's grin broadened. "I can work with that."

"But before you whisk our girl away, you'll eat. Sit down. There's plenty to go around." Aunt Faye skirted around them to set the massive tray of pancakes on the table just as Uncle Mark came into the room, clearly fresh from a shower himself.

"Mornin', Declan."

"Mornin', sir."

And so it went through the meal. Everyone lapsed into easy conversation, as if it was just another summer workday and Declan hadn't been out of their lives for more than a decade. Livia didn't say much. She was too busy splitting her attention between the pancakes and the occasional brush of Declan's leg against hers—something else that was a relic of times gone by. It still made her giddy, and by the time plates were cleared and the dishwasher loaded, she'd decided not to fight it.

So when Declan offered his hand and asked, "Ready to go?" Livia didn't even ask where. She simply curled her fingers around his and said, "Yes."

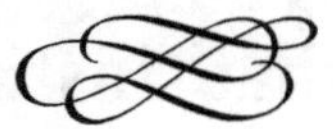

CHAPTER 8

"What are we doing today?"

Declan shut the driver's side door and came around to meet Livia where she stood on the downtown sidewalk. "It's not as fun as attending festival activities or walking down memory lane, but I need to meet with a realtor. I'm expected up here in less than a month, so I've got to find somewhere for us to live. Probably a short-term rental, because I can't fathom being able to close fast enough to buy. It's one of the things on my to do list that I've been putting off."

Everything that could be done outside business hours had been accomplished via late nights at the inn, fueled by an inadvisable amount of coffee in order to free his days up to spend with

Livia. He was definitely feeling the fact that he was no longer eighteen, but he wouldn't trade the last few days for anything in the world. Full days and evenings spent walking and talking about everything under the sun. Holding hands. Kissing. Touching in that instinctive, comfortable way. Being with Livia was easy. It had always been easy. But he didn't take it for granted this go round.

She slid her arms around his waist and beamed a sunny smile up at him. "I'd be happy to look at properties with you. I'm just happy to spend time with you right now."

She followed the declaration with a kiss that left Declan sighing, pulling her closer so she fit up against his chest like a puzzle piece sliding into place. This was perfection. She was perfection. The past few days with her were more than he'd expected to have in his wildest dreams.

Because she felt guilty for hanging out with him when she'd planned the trip to see family, they'd shared breakfast every morning with the Whittakers. He'd been surprised at their unequivocal welcome back to the fold. He hadn't expected such easy forgiveness, and he felt guilty for staying away from them for so long when they'd always been such good, wonderful people to him. Declan didn't overlook the fact that they seemed completely onboard with the idea of him wooing Livia all over again, and he appreciated their support. Because he was greedy and wanted so much more from her than a few stolen days.

At the sound of someone's whistle, they broke apart with a laugh.

"I keep forgetting we're in public."

Declan took her hand. "You don't hear me complaining." Though he definitely wanted the opportunity for some privacy that didn't involve the backseat of his car.

They strode down the street to Bradford Realty. A few minutes later, they were ushered down the hall and into an office. A smartly dressed woman in a pantsuit rose from behind the desk and offered a manicured hand. "I'm Magnolia Bradford. How can I help y'all today?"

He shook, appreciating her firm, businesslike grip. "Declan Callahan. And this is Livia Applewhite. We're looking for houses."

Livia was staring. "I'm sorry. I just have to say your eye makeup is absolutely stunning."

Declan focused in. Her dark eyes really did look lovely with… whatever she'd done to them. A faint sense of unease set in as it occurred to him that Scarlett wasn't far off from probably wanting to wear makeup. What if he had to learn about that, too?

Magnolia grinned, and a couple of dimples popped in her medium brown cheeks. "Thank you! What kind of house are y'all looking for?"

Too late, Declan realized he'd made it sound like they were a couple looking for a house together. But Livia didn't correct the assumption. Was that significant? He wanted it to be. They'd talked about almost everything the past few days, but she hadn't said another word about making a change in her life. Not since that initial mention of being unhappy in Wishful. He'd been too afraid to bring up the idea of her moving here to give them a real shot. That felt like he'd be pushing too hard, too fast, even though it was what he really wanted. But maybe…

Realizing he still hadn't answered, he focused back on Magnolia. "Three bedrooms, two baths. Decent yard, but not gigantic."

She began scribbling notes on a legal pad. "Closer to town or out some?"

"Closer. Potentially within walking distance of downtown. The area of Nashville we're in now has a lot of stuff close. My daughter and I like to walk around and get a meal or see whatever there is to see. And I don't want to be too far out because I'll already have to drive a bit to get to work at the Old Mill."

"Oh! You're taking over as manager of the Guild for Maggie."

"I am. I'm one of the droves of Joan's kids."

"Coming home. Love to see it. What is it you do, Livia?"

"I'm a librarian."

"Oh, will you be joining the staff here to work with Donna Black?"

Livia glanced quickly at him, then away again. "That's kind of up in the air at the moment. I don't know exactly what I'll be doing."

Declan wanted to whoop. That was as much as an admission that she was actually thinking about moving! But he needed to keep it cool and no pressure, see how the day went.

They spent hours with Magnolia, looking at house after house, in town, and out. There were move-in ready houses and fixer uppers. Some had yards that were too big. Some too small. Some were too far out. Some were too close in. Not that there was too much rowdy at Elvira's Tavern, but Declan would just as soon not be right on the other side of their fence. He was starting to feel like Goldilocks, being too picky by half, when they pulled up in front of the two-story Victorian behind Magnolia's car.

In the passenger's seat, Livia lit up. "Oh! It reminds me of home. My house in Wishful—my parent's house where I grew up—is a big Victorian farmhouse. It's bigger than this, but it's got similar bones."

"Reminds me of home, too." Joan's home was a three-story Victorian that had been in her family for generations. She'd made it a warm, welcoming home for so many fosters, over so many years, she'd started calling it The Misfit Inn. His sisters had converted it into a proper inn after her death. That place had always been what the word "home" conjured in his mind.

Three blocks down from Main Street, the house was painted dark gray with white trim that was peeling in places. Not the color he'd have chosen, but paint could be changed. There was a porch across the front, with a swing at one end and a big bay window at the other.

"I saved the best for last. This one's a short sale, so it might actually suit your timeline for getting up here next month, depending on your funding approval." Magnolia led them inside and began giving them the tour.

Like many of the others, the house was a fixer

upper. There was dated wallpaper and oak cabinets that had clearly been installed during the eighties. Brass fixtures dated the place even more. But the bones were good. That bay window was in the dining room and had a window seat Scarlett would love. Built-ins surrounded it, and he could just see them all full of books. Most of the changes that were needed were cosmetic. Paint and hardware, new light fixtures.

"The floors are the original hardwood," Magnolia explained. "The current owners found them beneath the carpet and had planned to refinish them but didn't get around to it before they left. They're in good shape, so that wouldn't be a difficult job. And of course, you'd have an in with Porter at Mountainview Construction."

The kitchen had a back door that led out into a comfortably sized yard that was already fenced. The whole property was just over half an acre, with old-growth trees shading the house. There was more landscaping work that needed doing, but he was no stranger to that. It was easy to see family cookouts on the patio back here, with a picnic table and a passel of kids and a sloppy dog. And Livia stepping out of the house with a tray of food to go on a big ass grill.

As they finished the tour and thanked Magnolia, Livia asked, "Would the owners mind if we just sat here on the swing for a bit?"

She smiled. "Take your time. If y'all decide you want to make an offer, you let me know. You've got my card."

With a little wave, she strolled down the front walk and got into her car. He and Livia moved to sit on the porch swing. He slipped his arm around her, sighing as she snuggled into him as if she'd been doing it every day for years.

"The sunset would be gorgeous from this spot," she murmured.

"It will be."

She straightened a little. "You're going to make an offer?"

"I think so. The house is perfect. Or will be, with a little TLC. And the short sale is certainly attractive under the circumstances. If we can avoid having to move twice, I definitely want to."

"Do you want to go flag down Magnolia? I can still see her car at the end of the street."

Declan tugged her back into the circle of his arm. "It'll keep for a little while longer. I want to enjoy sitting here with you."

He set them to rocking, and they both dreamed.

She'd fit here. With him. With them. A central

part of his life with Scarlett. Declan wanted that more than he'd wanted anything since… well, since her. Maybe it was time to start putting things in place to make that happen.

Her stomach was the one that growled first, with his right behind.

Livia laughed. "I guess a very late lunch is in order."

"I certainly owe you a meal for your very patient tagging along on a less than exciting task."

"It was fun helping you look at property."

He hoped she'd been thinking about how she could fit into them, too.

They rose, and he turned to face her, taking both her hands in his. "Do you have a date for the Harvest Ball on Saturday?"

Amusement made her eyes shine. "No. I hadn't expected to go, so I don't have a dress either."

"Can you get one?" Not that it mattered. She could wear a burlap sack, and he'd still think she was beautiful.

Her thumbs stroked across the backs of his hands. "I feel like I can make that happen. If I don't find anything in the shops, Abbey probably has something I can borrow."

"Then will you go with me? An official,

grownup date?" Nerves danced in his belly. She could say no and that might be the end of this. She might not want to open the door to going beyond what they'd had when they were young.

But her smile bloomed slow and sweet, like an apple blossom. "I'd love to go on an official, grown-up date with you."

Damn if he didn't feel like he'd just won the lottery.

* * *

WHEN LIVIA HAD ACCEPTED Declan's invitation to the Harvest Ball, she'd imagined getting some good girl time in with Abbey to shop for a dress. Despite Abbey's blatant enthusiasm for the rekindling of her relationship with Declan, Livia still felt guilty for ignoring her. But her cousin had been up half the night with off-and-on Braxton-Hicks contractions, so she'd been ordered off her feet and was grumpy about it. After promising to video call from the dressing room with any options, Livia headed into Eden's Ridge to see what there was on offer. Given the size of the town, she didn't have high hopes and fully expected to end up driving into Johnson City, nearly an hour away. But it was worth the effort to make a sweep if it might save her the trip.

Being on her own felt strange. She'd been joined at the hip with Declan since the fair. Today was the first day they hadn't shared breakfast with the family. He was off taking care of grownup things related to his upcoming move, with a promise they'd get together later. She trusted he meant it. Their time together this week had put her doubts to rest. She'd avoided family breakfast today, not wanting to face questions they might have for what came next. They were all wondering. So was she, no matter how hard she was trying to simply stay in the moment.

Thinking too far ahead felt dangerous. At eighteen, they'd planned a whole life together and none of it had come to fruition. If the glow of possibility illuminated every interaction they had, well, she was fighting the urge to dream.

Mostly.

She'd failed at that yesterday when they'd been at the house, too easily able to see a shared life there. Declan felt it, too. She knew he did. But that was getting well ahead of themselves. They weren't simply an unattached man and woman anymore. He had to think of his daughter first. As he should. But, at least for a few more days, Livia had him to herself.

She intended to make the most of it.

A cold front had moved in overnight. Livia hunched into her coat as she locked the car and began the walk toward Main Street. From here, she was only about a quarter mile from the little Victorian. Declan had called Magnolia to put in an offer last night and was starting the process of getting his financing in order today. With luck, he'd hear by the end of the week whether the sellers accepted. And then… well, they'd see, she supposed. They wouldn't be able to avoid having a serious discussion about whether they were going to try for a different kind of future to-gether and what all that might entail. But for a little while longer, she just wanted to enjoy the now.

"Livia!"

Her head jerked up to find a smiling blonde unlocking a shopfront door. The woman looked dimly familiar.

Even as Livia scrolled through her brain, trying to identify her, she touched a hand to her chest. "Maggie."

The lightbulb went off. "You're one of De-clan's sisters."

"Yes. We met years ago, when you and Declan dated the first time."

Livia flashed an apologetic smile. "It's been a long time."

"That it has. Step on inside. Let's talk out of the cold."

"Oh, I—um—"

But Maggie didn't wait for her assent, just opened the door and disappeared.

Not wanting to be rude, Livia followed. It did feel nice to be out of the wind. Maggie crossed over to the exposed brick wall to turn on a light. Livia didn't know what she'd expected, but the empty, cavernous space wasn't it. The shop was long and deep, clearly stretching from the front all the way to the alley that no doubt ran behind the building. The scarred wood floors were dusty, and she could just discern the outline where shelves or counters used to be.

"What is this place?"

"Used to be a shoe store, and I think maybe a barber shop during one point of its lifetime. Hasn't been anything for many years, but I'm hoping to change that."

Curious, Livia turned to face her. "Declan tells me you run a small business incubator. We have one of those in my hometown that's done quite well."

Maggie brightened. "Oh, that's right! You're from Wishful. I've actually toured that one to get a sense of how they set it up and operate."

Relaxing at the common ground, she moved closer. "Then you've met Tess Campbell."

"Yes! She's become a friend of mine. She was a great resource in helping get our incubator off the ground. Because Eden's Ridge is smaller, we're playing with a slightly different model here, focusing on what kinds of businesses can be combined to allow for shared spaces and overhead. It lowers the risk for both partners involved, and generally makes both businesses more sustainable, which is better for our overall growth."

"So you're kind of like a matchmaker for businesses?"

"Exactly. People come to us pitching their ideas, and we try to help find a partner or partners to pair them with, and then give them the necessary training and hand-holding on the business side of things, in order to bring both concepts to fruition. And we also help with start-up grants. So far, we've had some pretty great results. Now that Declan's going to be taking over management of the Artisan Guild, I'll have some more time to put into finding businesses to fill the vacant spaces downtown."

Intrigued despite herself, Livia made no move to leave. "Like what?"

"Well, today I'm meeting with Hope Mac-Intosh. She and her brother Ford started Temptation Vineyards. The vineyard itself is doing okay, but it's a bit off the beaten path, so they're looking at the feasibility of a space in town so that people could try their wares. I'm not sure if a tasting room would make it here on its own. A lot of things wouldn't, which is why a lot of the focus of our incubator is on partnering complimentary businesses. The dual business approach helps defray overhead for both, so there's less burden on each. But I confess, I haven't figured out what would pair well with a tasting room."

"A bookstore." The words popped out before Livia could think better of it.

Now it was Maggie who looked intrigued. "You think?"

"I mean, you'd more often see a bookstore paired with a tea shop or coffeeshop. But it could work with a tasting room. Bookstores, as they used to be, have taken a real hit with the rise of ebooks and online retailers, so you'd have to have one that was really about selling the experience of books rather than the books themselves. The smell and feel of paper, the ability to sit down and open a book in your hands. Being able to browse the stacks. Getting hand-sold recommendations from someone who knows the genres. Events." With every word, her focus sharpened as the vision began to build itself.

Unable to help herself, she began to pace, imagining the room filled with shelves and tables and comfortable furniture. "A good bookstore is central to its town. They're gathering places. They can be event spaces, places for groups to meet. Book clubs. Knitting circles. All that could easily pair with wine. Depending on how it shook out, you'd see most of the foot traffic coming in during the day for the bookstore, and then the store would shift gears to wine for the evenings. You'd want someone trained in both, probably, with the ability to sell both for the bookstore and do tastings for walk-ins, but that would eliminate the need for a full-time person for each, at least until the model proved viable. Or you could go a step further and make it a wine bar instead of a tasting room."

Hands clapped and a new voice called, "Sold!"

Livia turned to find Maggie standing with a

new woman, with a riot of curly brown hair that had clearly been a victim of the blustery day.

Maggie herself was nodding. "Yes, to all of that! Are you in the book business?"

"Tangentially. I'm a librarian."

"Well, if you ever decide to jump to the sales side of the fence, let me know. I'd love to see an application from you for the business incubator."

"I don't have any business experience." She'd spent her whole career in the public sector.

"That's the whole point of the incubator. To help you with the skills you don't have in order to bring your vision to life."

Not sure what to do with that, Livia murmured, "I'll keep that in mind." She glanced at the new arrival again, not sure how to make a graceful exit.

Maggie waved a hand. "Where have my manners gone? Hope, I'd like you to meet Livia Applewhite. Livia, Hope McIntosh of Temptation Vineyards."

Hope beamed. "Declan's girl."

Livia paused, hand outstretched. "Uh…"

The brunette laughed. "Word gets around."

"So it would seem." Needing to escape, Livia began to back toward the door. "I'm gonna get out of your way so y'all can talk business. It was nice to meet you, Hope, and good to see you again, Maggie."

"Same! And I hope you'll put in an application."

"Oh, yes please," Hope exclaimed. "I'd *love* not to have to go all the way to Johnson City or give all my money to the clutches of the great 'zon. And the pairing of books with our wine could be epic."

"I'll think about it. Meanwhile, do either of you have a suggestion for where I can get a dress for the Harvest Ball? That was the whole reason I came to town this morning."

"Absolutely."

Armed with Maggie's directions, Livia bid them both farewell and headed down the street toward the dress shop. But the whole way there, she couldn't help but dream of possibilities.

CHAPTER 9

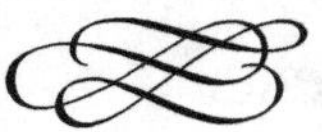

"Wait! Wait!"

Declan paused, hand on the front door of the inn.

"You can't go like that," Ari insisted.

He glanced down at his gray suit. It wasn't bespoke, but it had been serviceable enough for the infrequent occasions he'd needed one. And he'd even put on a tie and shined his shoes. "Why not?"

She held up a hand. "Don't move."

On a sigh, he waited as she disappeared into the kitchen. He was itching to get to the orchard to see Livia again. She'd been tied up most of the day hanging with Abbey, and he'd been occupied himself, trying to set some things in motion.

Staying away had still been torture. The knowledge that his time with her was limited made every second precious. He didn't want to waste a single one.

Ari reappeared with something in her hands. "You have to take these."

"Flowers?"

She reached up to fasten a boutonnière in his buttonhole. "Daffodils are for new beginnings. It's good luck. There's a corsage for Livia, too."

Declan couldn't stop the smile. "You really are a romantic, aren't you? Thanks. This is really sweet."

Ari winked. "The sweet helps make up for the nosy."

"Ah, so *that's* how you get away with everything."

She tapped a finger to the side of her nose and handed over the corsage in a little plastic box. "Go woo your lady."

Saluting, he headed for the car, an extra spring in his step.

The closer he got to the orchard, the twitchier he got. He didn't recall ever being this nervous before a date, not even when he'd been a teenager going to a school dance. Then again, it hadn't felt like his life was riding on prom.

I don't have to have everything figured out today. I just have to convince her to take a chance on us again.

He pulled up to Kyle and Abbey's house and slid out of the car, smoothing down his tie. The door swung open before he got to it. But it was Abbey, rather than Livia, framed in the entrance. She looked him over, her gaze lingering on the corsage box in his hand. With a satisfied nod, she opened the door wider. "You'll do."

Declan stepped inside, taking in her yoga pants and blousy shirt. "You're not going tonight?"

"Much as I want to, there is no dress on earth that will look like anything other than a tent on me right now, and the idea of dress shoes makes me want to weep. I'm sitting this one out."

Kyle emerged from somewhere in the back, sliding an arm around his wife and dropping a kiss to her head. "We're going to have a nice night at home eating ice cream and popcorn and bingeing her favorite movies."

"There are worse ways to spend an evening." Declan wondered if he'd ever get the chance to just cuddle up with Livia on the sofa and do exactly that.

"You come bearing flowers? That was a nice move," Kyle observed.

"That's got Ari written all over it," Abbey declared. "It's still a nice move."

"Pretty sure she's bucking to be a professional matchmaker when she grows up. I'm a little afraid of her long-term influence on Scarlett."

"Three words," Kyle said. "Force of nature."

The sound of footsteps on the stairs had them all looking up. Her slim feet were encased in those strappy shoes with sky high heels that were impractical as hell and made men stupid. Which was probably the point. Declan's gaze slid up from them, taking in slim, smooth legs and a fitted dress that hit her just above the knees and shimmered like stars in the night sky. Her pale hair was swept up in some kind of complicated knot, leaving her long, lovely neck bare. Lust pooled low in his belly. This wasn't the girl he'd fallen for all those years ago. This was a woman grown, and he wanted her.

"Wow."

Color rose in Livia's cheeks. "You clean up pretty well yourself."

That uncharacteristically shy smile had him moving forward, opening the box. "This is for you."

For a moment, her face blanked. "You got me a corsage?"

Declan pulled it back. "Was that wrong? If it doesn't go with the dress, you don't have to wear it."

Her hand shot out and settled on his arm, her face suffusing with pleasure. "No! It's perfect."

You're perfect.

He kept the words to himself as he set the box aside and tied the corsage onto her wrist. If his fingers lingered on the pulse point jumping there, he wasn't going to apologize. He needed to touch her, to make sure this vision before him was real. Livia's breath caught at the contact, and her gaze lifted to his.

A camera clicked, the sound breaking the tension of the moment. They both glanced over to see Abbey with her phone in hand.

"You two are adorable. I had to document."

Livia's mouth quirked. "I'll be sure to text if I'm out after curfew, Mom."

Well, didn't that just give Declan some ideas? Reining them in, he offered his arm. "Shall we?"

She slid her arm through his, and he decided that, for tonight at least, everything was right in his world.

By the time they got to the ball, people were streaming into the building, dressed in varying degrees of finery. Declan found a parking space and climbed out, hurrying around to open Livia's door. She took his hand and slid out, taking in the multi-story stone building set into the mountain slope.

"Welcome to the Eden's Ridge Artisan Guild and Education Center, otherwise known as the Old Mill, because the other is a mouthful."

"This is where you'll be working?"

"Yep. My brother Porter and his wife Maggie were the brain trust behind all this. The mill itself was built by one of my foster mom's ancestors, and they elected to convert it to house a maker's space and classrooms. The guild itself has been around for a while, but this really formalized the arrangement, giving them somewhere to showcase their wares and teach their assorted crafts." They stepped through the tall double doors on the second floor and into the main level of the building. "This floor has a huge open space that gets used for events like this. My brother Kendrick's wedding reception was here last weekend. And they host weekly jam nights with local musicians during the time of year the weather isn't conducive to having them outside."

She seemed to be trying to look everywhere at once. There was plenty to look at with the cafe lights and streamers crisscrossing the high ceiling and the myriad of tables with harvest-themed centerpieces around the edge of the dance floor.

"And you'll be organizing all that?"

"I will. Maggie's been pulling double duty, so she's happy to finally hand it off to someone else so she can focus on her true passion."

"The business incubator."

He glanced down at her in surprise. "Exactly. Good memory."

"I ran into her downtown the day I went dress shopping, and we had a chat about it."

"Oh?"

"She's a formidable woman, your sister."

"She is that," Declan agreed, though he wondered what Livia meant.

Before he could ask, the woman herself hailed them. "Declan! Livia! It's so good to see you both."

"You, too, sis." He pulled her in for a quick hug.

Livia gestured around them. "Declan's been telling me about your brainchild here. It's certainly something."

Maggie laughed. "I can only claim credit for the idea. My husband was the one who brought it to life."

"Where is Porter, anyway?" Declan asked.

"Oh, he and Xander are helping carry in some

extra kegs for the bar. Ari's running herd on Athena's boys, and the three of them are watching all the babies so we can have a night out."

His attention snagged on that detail. "So nobody's watching the inn?"

"We blocked off the guest list to family only for the weekend, and all of us are here."

Which meant the house was empty. No brothers. No sisters. No well-intentioned matchmaking teenager. Livia tucked her arm through his, pressing subtly against him, and he wondered if she was thinking what he was.

"Livia, have you given any further thought to our discussion?"

Declan focused back on the conversation, curious what this was about.

"A little. It would be a big change."

"What kind of big change?" he asked.

Eyes a little uncertain, Livia admitted, "A bookstore. Maggie thinks there's an opportunity for one here, through the business incubator. Maybe in conjunction with a tasting room or wine bar."

"Hope adored the idea. She couldn't stop gushing after you left the other day. A full on wine bar hadn't been on her radar, but since you mentioned it, she's exploring the possibility."

Declan tried to rein in his excitement. "Obviously, my vote would be yes."

"It would be a big commitment."

He understood she wasn't just talking about the business but about them, and he was beyond ready to stop tiptoeing around what he felt. If he didn't take some kind of leap, he'd lose her again.

From the stage, a jazz band struck up "Dream a Little Dream".

Sliding his hand down to the small of Livia's back, he took a step back. "If you'll excuse us, I'm gonna steal my date for a dance."

"Enjoy the night, you two."

As his sister disappeared into the crowd, Declan steered Livia toward the dance floor, pulling her into his arms. Her body hummed with tension.

Wanting to reassure, he pulled her closer, stroking a hand down her back. "I'm not going to push you on this."

Her gray eyes lifted to his. "You aren't?"

"You don't like making snap decisions. You prefer to consider all the angles. That's something I learned about you back when, and I still appreciate it, so I get it's hard. There are a million and one things to factor in. So let's just keep things simple tonight. You. Me. The music. Or…"

"Or?"

Bending closer to her ear, he murmured, "Or, we take advantage of the completely empty inn and finish what we started all those years ago."

He felt the hitch of her breath.

Shock? Desire? Both?

When her gaze came back to his, her eyes were bottomless pools. "I vote for door number two."

* * *

THE PORCH LIGHTS of the grand Victorian shone with a cheery glow against the cool winter night. Livia climbed the front steps, her fingers laced with Declan's, her heart drumming a skittering tattoo. She remembered waiting for him all those years ago, knowing they'd been headed exactly for this and wanting him more than her next breath. There'd been nerves, too, about what was to come. Not from doubts. Never that. But from worry over not knowing what to expect. They'd fooled around a little before, but she'd been otherwise untouched. She'd wanted him to be the first.

She was older now, maybe wiser, and there were still nerves. She knew her body and understood the dance. Would it be as good as she'd imagined, without the rose-colored glow of first love coloring the night?

At the door, he brought their joined hands to his lips, pressing a kiss to her knuckles before he slid his key into the lock.

Livia's heart did a little swoon.

It's not first love. Not now. It's something more, and you know it.

She'd known it that night at the fair, as all those old feelings stretched and woke with his kiss. They'd only grown stronger, day by day, as they'd reconnected. Yes, they were both different, with new fears and a caution they hadn't possessed at eighteen. But underneath, at the core, they were still who they'd always been. And that was why she was here, why she'd chosen the "or." Because she still wanted him more than her next breath. Because no matter what happened tomorrow, she wanted tonight.

They stepped into the house, pausing to listen in the foyer.

"Hello?" Declan's voice rang out, strangely loud. When no answer came, he shrugged. "Seems like it really is empty. It's kind of weird, actually. I can't recall this house ever being empty."

"Then let's make the most of it." Aware tonight could as easily be their first *and* last time, Livia rose up to take his mouth.

His arm came around her, drawing her flush to his body, his hum of pleasure vibrating against her chest. His voice shook a little as he pulled back. "Not here. Upstairs. In case."

She was definitely not here for any interruptions. "Lead the way."

With every step, anticipation mounted, and when they stepped into his third-floor bedroom, she fairly quaked with it. Until he stopped just inside the door.

One hand went to the back of his neck, rubbing awkwardly. "I, um, hadn't booked the room with this in mind."

Livia took in the twin beds and understood he'd shared this space with Scarlett. His daughter. The necessary center of his world. He'd be going to get her tomorrow. Livia had no idea how that might change things. While they'd talked of Scarlett often this week, there'd been no discussion of introducing Livia. An abundance of caution on his part, or a reluctance to look too far into the future?

Don't overthink it. He wants you to stay in Eden's

Ridge. That implies that, at some point, the two parts of his world will collide.

Turning, she laid a hand on his chest. "I think we can manage. Unless you feel weird now and want to change your mind?"

Declan drew her in, hip-to-hip, so she could feel the erection straining his suit pants. "Does that feel like I've changed my mind?"

"Just checking."

His hand skimmed the hair back from her face. "If I'd known we'd have the chance to do this, I'd have rustled up a little romance."

"Oh?"

"Mmm." He pressed a kiss to her temple, then lower, to the apple of her cheek. "Candles. Flowers. Maybe some champagne, now that we're both legal." With every word, he pressed another kiss to her skin, trailing down, down the slope of her neck and making her shudder. "It's what I had planned out for our weekend at the cabin."

Her hands tightened on his shirt as he lingered on the valley of her collarbone. "You did?"

His fingers went to the zipper of her dress and began to slowly inch it down. "I did. I wanted to make your first time special. Perfect."

The picture he painted was full of sweetness and beauty. And a part of her grieved that they hadn't made it that far. But the grief was overtaken by sensation as he continued to explore each new inch of exposed skin with his lips. No matter their unfulfilled intentions from the past, they were together. Now.

Dragging her languorous eyes open, she met his gaze. "That would have been lovely, but I don't need all the trappings. I just need you."

He murmured her name and took her mouth in a deep, drugging kiss that put an end to any conversation. Hands found their way to flesh, shedding layers as they kissed and kissed, as if they had all the time in the world. As if this were a beginning, not an end. And when he laid her back on the bed, following her down, Livia gave herself over to the hope and the need.

Declan's mouth stayed on hers as his clever hands explored every dip and curve. And when he parted her folds and found her wet, she pressed her hips against his hand, seeking more. He gave—oh mercy; he gave. Under his ruthlessly patient ministrations, her body wound tighter and tighter, until something inside her snapped, and she rode that long, lovely crest of release she knew was only the beginning.

Blinking her eyes open, she found him staring

down at her, his lips curved into a self-satisfied smile. "Hello again, gorgeous."

"Hi."

"You're stunning when you come apart for me."

"It'll be even better when you're with me." His eyes drooped as she threaded her fingers in his hair. "I need you, Declan. Don't make me wait anymore."

He kissed her again, fast and hard, before disappearing. Before she could protest, she heard the rip of foil. Then he was back, one knee between hers as he crawled up from the foot of the bed. She spread her legs, making room for him, and watched as he settled that long, lean body of his over her.

His lips were gentle as they brushed over hers. "Are you sure?"

She hooked a hand behind his neck. "I've never been more sure of anything."

Their gazes locked and held as he slipped slowly inside her. At last. *At last.* The friction and fullness were delicious and perfect, as she'd known it would be. Staring into his familiar hazel eyes, she admitted the truth she'd been denying. She couldn't fight this. It was him for her. It had always been him, and she refused to let him go this time.

Surging up, she took his mouth, wrapping tighter around him to pull him deeper into her body, her heart. His answering kiss tasted of fierceness, with an edge of fever and frenzy as he began to move. Joy and pleasure built between them, a rising storm that wiped away worry and doubt. And in her newfound freedom, she leapt off the cliff to fly, pulling him over behind her.

CHAPTER 10

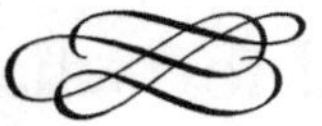

$\mathcal{N}$othing in Declan's life had ever been as glorious as being wrapped up with a naked and sated Livia Applewhite, feeling her sweat-slicked skin cooling against his, her hands trailing lazily over his back and shoulders. He wanted to stay here forever, buried inside her until he'd recovered enough for an encore. But as he well knew, there were practicalities to be dealt with.

"Be right back." With one last lingering kiss, he carefully pulled out and went to dispose of the condom.

She was waiting for him with slumberous eyes when he returned. "Come back to bed."

"Gladly." He crawled back in beside her, wrapping her close, so he could stroke the dip of her waist, along the curve of her hip and around to explore the firm flesh of her backside.

Chest to chest, he felt the thud of her heart slowing against his. A thousand and one fantasies bloomed in his head for what they could do in a bigger bed or against a wall or on a counter... But right now, in this moment, he didn't mind the narrow bed and the necessity of staying tangled up so neither of them crashed off the side of the mattress.

Livia nuzzled into the crook of his neck. "This was worth the wait."

He couldn't disagree. Oh, he had no doubt they'd have been good together at eighteen. Young love would've made it so. But he didn't know if he'd have appreciated it quite so much for the precious thing it was.

Or maybe he would have, and it would've broken him even more.

"I'm glad we didn't get to this before."

She stiffened and began to shove away.

Declan just tightened his grip. "It's not because it wasn't amazing. But because if we had crossed this line, having to let you go would have hurt that much worse. And it damn near killed me as it was."

A furrow appeared between her brows as she settled back against him. "Why did you let me go?"

"Scarlett." That had and always would be his answer. His daughter came first.

"I know you had to be there for your daughter. You wouldn't have been the boy I fell in love with if you'd walked away. But you didn't have to go back to Bridget. I would have supported you."

Hearing her put into words the thing he'd been too afraid to ask at the time had a whole host of what-ifs swirling in his brain. But he wrestled them back. No point. It was over and done.

"That would have been an enormous amount of pressure on a very new relationship. I don't know if we would have survived it. Asking you to take on me as a single dad at nineteen? I couldn't do that to you. I knew going into it, because of my own parents, what that would be like. Not enough time, not enough resources, not enough education. Definitely not enough money. There was never enough of anything. That wasn't what I promised you."

"Did you think so little of me? That I wouldn't want you if we deviated from the plan?"

"No! Never that. But if we'd been able to stick

it out, it would have been an enormous stress on our relationship. Especially with what came after, and all the challenges of a special needs child. You wouldn't have gotten a normal college experience. I certainly didn't. I ended up not going to UT, as planned. I finished my degree, eventually, but it was mostly online while working full time trying to support us all. I just didn't think it was fair to you. And maybe I didn't trust that we could make it because I couldn't imagine anybody choosing to stay through all of that." His wife certainly hadn't, and he still bore the scars of her betrayal. "We were so young."

Livia lay silent and still for a long while. "We're not so young now."

There was something in her tone that had everything in him coiling tight with some mix of hope and dread. "What are you saying?"

She took a deep breath and pushed herself up to look into his face. Her gray eyes were dark as they searched his. "We just found each other again. I don't want to walk away from this. Not again. Because it's you, Declan. It's always been you."

Emotion clogged his throat, because it had always been her for him, too. Unable to speak, he surged forward to kiss her again, communicating with his body what he couldn't force past his lips. He loved this woman. Had always loved this woman. He didn't know what he'd done to earn a second chance with her, but he wasn't about to waste it.

As her hands skated down his torso and lower to wrap around his cock, he realized he could absolutely go for round two.

Love, the wonder drug.

Bucking into her hand, he was just on the verge of urging her to straddle him when a text tone sounded from his phone. Scarlett.

She was with her grandparents. She was probably just bored. It could wait.

But the tone sounded again. And again in quick succession.

The father in him wouldn't let him ignore it.

"Put a pin in this for just a minute. I've got to check that."

Scrambling out of the bed, he searched the floor for his pants and dug out his phone, swiping open the screen.

As he read the series of texts, his heart clenched, and his stomach sank.

SCARLETT

Mom's here.

She's trying to take me with her.

Come. Hurry!

All the blood drained out of his head.

Livia sat up in bed, the covers pooling around her waist. "What's wrong?"

"I have to go. It's… It's Scarlett. Bridget's at her parents'. She's trying to take her."

"Oh my God." Livia threw the covers back and dove for her clothes. "Of course. Let's go."

Even as he thrilled to her ready defense, he was shaking his head. "No, I need to do this on my own." The last thing he wanted was for Livia to be exposed first-hand to Bridget's crazy. The woman poisoned everything she touched, and he wouldn't have her fucking things up again.

Livia paused as she fastened her bra, her face blanking.

Declan knew he'd hurt her, but he didn't have time to explain right now. He continued to drag on clothes. "I'm sorry. I'm sorry. I just I need to go deal with this on my own. I don't know how long it's going to take. But I'll be in touch tomorrow."

"Okay."

She'd pulled her dress back on by the time he

found his wallet and keys, and Declan realized he couldn't just leave her here. What kind of asshole would that make him? But the idea of having to drive all the way out to the orchard before leaving for Knoxville had panic unfurling in his chest.

Livia must've seen it in his face because she stepped up, cupping his cheek. "Don't worry about me. I'll find my own ride back to the farm. Go rescue Scarlett."

Loving her more than ever for not fighting him on this, Declan pressed one last kiss to her lips. "I'll be in touch tomorrow."

"Tomorrow."

With that one word echoing in his ears, he raced out.

* * *

THE SUN WAS SINKING below the horizon as Livia plucked the pages from the printer and retreated up to her room to proofread them. She'd already done that in the file on her computer, but she'd always preferred one last pass on paper. There was something different about holding a document in her hand with a handy dandy red pen, and it was yet one more delaying tactic. But half an hour later, she had to concede that the application was finished.

Because, of course, it was finished. Taking Maggie at her word, Livia had started on her business plan Sunday to distract herself from worry about Declan and Scarlett, this child she didn't even know. She'd worked on it off and on between visits with Abbey and the rest of the family as she'd waited for any word from him. Now Wednesday and come and gone and there'd been nothing. Nothing but this completed application that represented the dying hope she'd had for a new life.

What was the point of submitting it?

Declan had promised she'd hear from him tomorrow, and it had been four days without a word. He hadn't responded to any of her texts. She hadn't called in case he was in the middle of... who knew what? But even in the midst of whatever he was dealing with, how could he not have found a moment to send up a smoke signal or a flare or a simple text to say *Tied up. Will get back to you later*? Something to acknowledge that he was still alive? That everything was okay? That he still cared to keep their connection going?

Instead, she'd gotten silence.

God, that cut deep.

It was all too easy to remember how it had felt, going off to school at eighteen, missing out on most of her freshman year by refusing to go out, to meet people, to do anything, because she'd been so committed to waiting for him. So certain the boy she loved couldn't possibly have abandoned her. How foolish and stupid she'd been to wait for so long. To not read the writing on the wall for what it was. No, the situation hadn't been what she'd thought. There'd been no malice in his actions. But the end result was the same.

She was quicker on the uptake now, for whatever that was worth. No matter what Declan was dealing with, he didn't trust or value her enough to be a part of it. That told her everything she needed to know.

Hands trembling, she began opening drawers. When Abbey came in a few minutes later, she'd made it about halfway through, folding all the clothes she'd brought with her on the trip.

"Okay, hiding out to fold laundry is just sad. Why don't I call up the girls? Maybe we can all go up to Elvira's for supper."

The girls were, Livia knew, likely Declan's sisters. Did they know what was going on? Did she want to find out that he'd been in contact with them and not her? That would be just another twist of the knife.

"I don't think so." She set another pair of folded jeans on the pile.

With a sigh, Abbey sank into the chair at the desk, one hand on her exceptional baby bump. Her gaze landed on the application Livia had set to the side. "What's this?"

"It's nothing."

But her cousin was the nosy sort, so she picked it up and skimmed the first page. Her face lit up. "You're applying for the small business incubator?"

"No, I'm not."

Abbey paged through. "But this looks like a finished application."

Livia laid another neatly folded shirt on the stack, aware that there was no need for this level of precision in her packing preparations, but folding gave her something to do with her still shaking hands. "It's something that I was thinking about doing before."

"Before what?"

"Before Declan ghosted me again." There. She'd admitted the truth she'd been avoiding out loud.

Distress raced over Abbey's face. "Livia… We don't know what it is."

Needing to keep moving, she hauled her suitcase out from beneath the bed. "It's been four days. I know he has to deal with whatever the hell is going on. But he said he'd be in contact tomorrow and it's been *four days*. Complete radio silence. He hasn't responded to anything. Not even to say *I can't talk right now*. Nothing."

"But—"

"No, Abbey!" As the tidal wave of emotion began to crest, she hurled stacks of clothes into the bag, undoing all the careful work folding. "It's done. I told him how I felt after the ball Saturday. After we…" After they'd slept together and he'd rocked her world. "He didn't respond in kind." And there'd been time before the texts came in. Not a lot, but some. He'd kissed her instead. To shut her up? To distract her? Because he didn't know what to say?

"I am not going to sit around, waiting forever, like I did twelve years ago. Message received. I can't be here anymore, Abs. I'm going home."

"Honey, you don't know that's what's going on. You know he had to go deal with that whole situation with Scarlett."

"I know." She dragged in a breath, searching

for a calm she absolutely didn't feel. "I know Scarlett has to come first. I get that she's his daughter, his child. That's exactly as it should be. But I'm not willing to come last. I am not willing to be an afterthought. I deserve better." And just once, she wished someone could love her like that.

"You're right. You absolutely do. But there has to be some other explanation. I just can't fathom Declan doing this to you again."

"There probably is an explanation. But at the end of the day, even if it's unintentional, I'm not a part of his everyday world, and he doesn't trust me enough or think of me enough to change that. So I'm done. I'm going home in the morning. It's been great to see you and I wish things had turned out differently. I wish I was better company. I wish that everything had unfolded like we both thought it would. But it didn't. And I'm done waiting."

With pointed deliberation, she stepped to her cousin and plucked the application from her fingers, dropping it into the trash, along with her hope that this second chance would be anything more than the resolution of old business.

CHAPTER 11

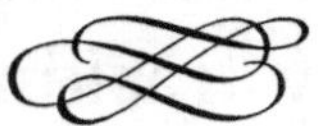

*D*eclan wasn't sure he'd ever been happier to see home than he was when he pulled up to the old Victorian late Friday afternoon. Exhaustion practically bled out of every pore, but the dumpster fire of his week had been extinguished. Finally. He hadn't known when they'd be arriving, but Pru had assured him they'd have a room ready, no matter when. Thank God for family.

Scarlett dozed in the passenger seat, finally able to rest for the first time since the weekend. As he took in the shadows beneath her eyes, temper stirred anew at his ex-wife. She'd terrified their daughter. And all Bridget had talked about when she'd been confronted was how hurt she was by Scarlett's rejection. As if she hadn't been rejecting Scarlett in big ways and small for years.

It took a few moments for Declan to lock down the rage again before he reached out to touch his daughter's shoulder. As her eyes fluttered open, instantly tracking to his, he signed, "We're here."

On a yawn and a stretch, she unfastened her seatbelt. "I'm hungry."

"I expect we can rustle up something in the kitchen."

Neither of them knocked before stepping inside.

"Welcome to The Misfit Inn. How can I— You're back!" Ari leapt up from the reception desk in the corner of the foyer and rushed around to fold Scarlett into a hug.

The immediate offering of comfort had Declan's throat going tight. He had to swallow twice before he could speak. "So we are. Where's your mom?"

Over Scarlett's head, Ari sobered, her expression far more adult and aware than any sixteen-year-old ought to be. "Kitchen. Athena and Kennedy are here, too."

"Thanks."

Tucking Scarlett close, Ari smiled down.

"Why don't you come with me while they catch up on all the boring stuff?"

"Do you have snacks? I'm starved."

"It happens we just finished filming an episode of *The Misfit Kitchen* this afternoon. There are leftovers in the studio kitchen. C'mon."

Blessing Ari for her intervention, Declan made his way into the kitchen, where three of his four sisters were clearly in conference with Flynn around the big farmhouse table.

"You're home!" Pru scrambled up and crossed to fold him into a hug.

Declan absorbed the embrace, momentarily pressing his cheek to the top of her head as he'd once done to Joan. "Thanks. I needed that. It's been a hell of a week."

Kennedy was next, giving him a solid squeeze. "We've been worried."

"I know. But I didn't want to get into it until we had some kind of resolution." Because he hated dragging anyone else into his mess, and he despised not having clear answers.

"Sit," Athena ordered. "I'll make coffee."

"I won't say no. I should probably move the car, though. I just parked out front."

"I'll do it." Flynn held out his hands for the keys. "I'll grab your bags, too."

"Thanks, brother."

When he'd disappeared, Pru herded Declan to the table, while Athena began fussing with the coffeepot.

"Now what happened? Is Scarlett okay?" Pru's big brown eyes were worried as she resumed her seat.

"She's… going to be." Scrubbing both hands over his face, Declan tried to decide on the most concise way to tell the story. "Y'all know she was spending last week with Bridget's parents. It's the longest unsupervised visit they've ever had. Scarlett wasn't exactly excited about it, but it seemed like time to try it out. I didn't see the sense in punishing them by withholding their granddaughter, just because Bridget walked away. Up to now, they've been completely aboveboard, seeming to really want a relationship with Scarlett."

Athena handed over a steaming mug. "Until now?"

"Thanks. Apparently, Barbara—that's Bridget's mama—decided she just needed to unify the family again. Didn't consult with me or clear it first. She told Bridget Scarlett was there. Bridget showed up Saturday night and tried to take her."

At the chorus of gasps and curses, Declan

sipped at the coffee, feeling the warmth of the mug soak into his palms.

"Can she do that?" Kennedy asked.

"No. She gave up all custodial rights when Scarlett was little. We have a visitation plan technically in place, but when Bridget never adhered to it, I stopped putting Scarlett through the stress of even trying. She doesn't know her mom anymore, and sure as hell didn't want to go with her. Bridget tried to pull parental rank, as if I haven't told Scarlett what she can and can't do. So Scarlett locked herself in her room and barricaded the door until I could get there."

"Shit," Athena murmured.

"Yeah. I'll spare you the recount of the rip-roaring fight we had. So now Scarlett doesn't trust her grandparents, and neither do I. I've just spent the last week getting my attorney involved to make sure that Bridget understands there will be no visitation that is unsupervised. If that's something she actually wants, she has to fucking earn it. She has to show up and prove she truly wants to be in Scarlett's life. I refuse to put my kid through the stress of all this."

"Well, you're home now, and you know we'll all close ranks to keep Scarlett safe if Bridget should come around again. Lord knows, there are enough of us." Pru whipped out her phone. "Do you have a current photo of her? I'll send it out with instructions on the family group text."

Declan felt the corners of his mouth twitch into a semblance of a smile. "I'll see what I can come up with."

"Seriously, anything we can do," Kennedy assured him.

"Actually, I was hoping y'all could keep an eye on Scarlett for an hour or two. I need to run over to the orchard to fill Livia in on all this."

The three of them exchanged a look that had fresh tension coiling in his gut.

"What?"

Pru laid a hand over his. "Honey, Livia went home."

"She what? But she was supposed to be here through Sunday."

Kennedy offered something that was halfway between a sympathetic smile and a wince. "Abbey said she was really upset."

Declan shoved out of his seat and began to pace. "Damn it. Damn it. Damn it! Damn Bridget. I didn't text her. I didn't call her. It's just been nuts, and I wanted to explain the shit show in person. And I—Fuck, I didn't want Bridget's crazy to bleed in."

It was the exact same choice he'd made twelve years ago. Not to clue her in and tell her what was going on. Not to trust her to be able to handle it.

"Oh no. No, no, no. She's never going to want to talk to me again after this." Declan squeezed his eyes shut as the weight of his actions sank in.

This was how he'd lost her the first time. When he'd ghosted her out of his own cowardice.

"Don't you think that's a touch dramatic?" Athena asked.

"No. Because she thinks I've ghosted her again. And I don't blame her."

Tipping his head back, he blew out a long breath. "Maybe this is a sign from the Universe. Maybe she's better off without me."

"No, Daddy!" Scarlett tumbled into the room, Ari right behind. "You have to go after her. Mom already ruined things for you with Livia once. Don't let her do it again."

Declan looked down at his wonderful, brilliant, resilient daughter, who still wanted him to have the chance to be happy after everything she'd just been through. He pulled her in for a tight hug.

"How do you feel about a road trip to Mississippi?"

Scarlett grinned. "I get to pick the snacks."

* * *

"JACE IS WORRIED ABOUT YOU. So am I."

Livia looked up from the ocean of ribbon and wreath-making supplies she was organizing in advance of the insanity that was next week's official opening of their Christmas tree farm for the season. Her sister-in-law leaned against the doorway, eying her with that concerned look she and her brother had been wearing for days. "I'm fine."

Tara straightened and stepped inside. "You're clearly not. You cut your trip short, and ever since you got back, you've been super withdrawn. Jace doesn't want to pry, but I will. What happened in Tennessee?"

Dropping her gaze, Livia tried to find an answer that would put an end to this line of questioning. "I got some long-needed closure. I'll be all right."

And she would. Eventually. She had reason to know that heartbreaks did eventually heal.

Tara's lips pressed together in an obvious struggle not to push for more. Instead, she wrapped her arms around Livia in a hug. "I'm here if you want to talk."

For just a moment, she tipped her head to Tara's, taking the comfort. "Thanks."

At the sound of an engine outside, Austin hollered, "Tara, you're up!"

She released Livia with a sigh. "Duty calls." With one last worried look, she went to handle the customer.

In the weeks leading up to opening day the Friday after Thanksgiving, the farm was open for limited hours to allow locals to come tag the trees they wanted to cut. The entire family was rotating who handled giving the newcomers the spiel, filling out tags and handing them over. Equitable division of labor. Livia had been hiding out, organizing stock in the barn for their product side lines. She didn't want to see anyone.

Once she'd organized the wired ribbon in a wooden crate to her satisfaction, she moved on to sorting the bulk ornaments. In another couple of days, her evenings would be full of decorating live wreaths to sell during opening weekend. She preferred to have each element grouped by color family. Long experience had taught her that sped up the process.

The phone in her pocket vibrated. She hesitated for long moments, resisting the urge to race for it. With everything in her, she tried not to care who'd sent the text, tried not to give in to the lingering ember of hope that it would be Declan. But she still fumbled it out with shaking fingers.

ABBEY

> Check your email.

Before the disappointment had even settled, a second text came in.

> Don't get mad.

Bracing herself for the consequences of her cousin's interference, Livia switched over to her email program and found one from Maggie Reynolds Ingram.

"Abbey, what the hell did you do?"

She opened the email.

Dear Livia,

Abbey brought me your application. I've reviewed the business plan and discussed it with my colleague here at our small business incubator, and we both agreed it looks absolutely fantastic. Your bookstore would be an outstanding addition to Eden's Ridge, and I'm delighted to offer you a spot in our program. Further details about how it works are attached, but please reach out with any questions. I look forward to hearing from you.

Maggie

Livia closed her eyes. "Dammit, Abbey. You had no right."

This was just an extra twist of the knife. To give her the perfect way to make a life in Eden's Ridge—right after everything with Declan fell apart. She didn't think she could do it. Be in the same small town as him, knowing she wasn't enough. The worst of it was that, as she'd written the business plan, she'd allowed herself to get excited about the idea of getting away from her job at the library to do something else. Not just anything else, but to create a business that was truly a part of a community. Maybe she could do that somewhere other than Eden's Ridge, but it wouldn't be Wishful. They already had a bookstore and couldn't support another.

So she was back to feeling stuck again, with no idea how to get out.

"The prodigal returns early. I feel like that's not a good sign."

Livia turned to face Autumn, spotting Riley right behind. "What are y'all doing here?"

"I heard from Miss Maudie Bell, who heard from Miss Betty, who was in the hardware store while Jace was talking to Tyler yesterday. He mentioned you were home already," Riley explained.

"So we came out to check on you, since you basically snuck in under cover of darkness and didn't let us know you were home."

"I didn't sneak," Livia protested. "It wasn't even after sunset when I drove into town."

Autumn waved a hand. "Same difference." Her green eyes searched Livia's face. "What happened?"

"I really don't want to get into it."

Autumn moved in to cup her face. "Somebody put heartbreak in your eyes. Whose ass do we need to kick?"

"We'll get Liam and Judd to hold him down if we need to."

Livia huffed a laugh, appreciating their ready defense. "That's not necessary. I just had a blast from the past. It didn't end any better than it did the first time. Lesson learned. I got closure and came home to help get ready for opening season. That's it."

Autumn pulled her in for a hug. "I'm sorry. I wished romance for you, not this."

Livia squeezed back. "We don't always get what we wish for."

Riley took her turn. "Maybe you needed to clear the decks of old business to make room for something even better."

Because she knew they needed it, Livia managed a smile. "Here's hoping."

"Liv! This one's yours!"

At her brother's shout, she rolled her eyes. She didn't want to deal with people, didn't want to give the spiel. But she was home, doing the work. It was only fair that she split the duties. "Hold that thought. I'll be right back."

Stepping out of the barn, she moved toward the basket where they kept tags and markers, but stopped as she took in the familiar blue sedan and its even more familiar driver.

Declan slid out of the car, and she could feel his eyes on her even from this distance. The passenger door opened, and a little girl stepped out the other side. As the two of them crossed over, Livia's heart began to thud.

He was *here.* And she had no idea how to feel about it. He'd come all this way. That had to mean something. Maybe just that he knew he'd screwed up badly enough that it merited an apology in person. Maybe to give her a proper goodbye.

There were a million and one things she wanted to say, but most of them weren't appropriate to utter in front of Scarlett, so she settled on, "What are you doing here?"

"We got back to Eden's Ridge yesterday. My sisters told me you'd already come home."

As that was obvious, she said nothing.

He stopped about ten feet from her, clearly uncertain of his welcome. "I owe you an apology. Again. For going all incommunicado. That was an especially dickish move after... Well, what happened with us before."

Again, not wanting to say anything negative about him in front of his daughter, Livia merely inclined her head to acknowledge the point.

Scarlett tugged at his sleeve and began signing to him.

Tell her, Dad.

"Tell me what?"

Declan glanced up in surprise. "You speak ASL?"

"I can't claim to be fully fluent, but I'm adequate. There's a little boy who comes to story time at the library who is hearing impaired. I learned so he can enjoy the stories like everyone else."

"Well, aren't you just full of surprises?"

Because the question seemed rhetorical, she stayed silent, waiting.

His gaze tracked behind her, where no doubt Riley and Autumn had emerged from the barn, and her brother and likely the rest of her family had gathered for the show. "Can I talk to you in private?"

When she only folded her arms and waited, Declan nodded.

"Okay, audience it is, then." He wiped his palms on his jeans and took a step closer, looking her full in the eye. "The reason I didn't call or text either time wasn't because I don't trust you, or because I wanted to ghost you or to walk away. It's because my time with you was the only time in my life that was ever perfect, and I was afraid that if you saw the full extent of crazy and chaos that's my real world, that you'd decide I wasn't worth it."

The heart Livia had tried to harden squeezed hard. Not worth it? How the hell could he think that? Didn't he understand how amazing he was?

Then she stopped to really consider the question.

He hadn't been enough for his parents. Hadn't been enough for his ex-wife. He'd been forced to do everything himself. Well, maybe not every-thing. He'd had his foster family, but that wasn't the same as what she'd had.

She'd been surrounded by supportive friends and family all her life. Hell, a small army of them were at her back right now. No matter what decision she made here today, they'd be there to support her and help her through it.

Declan hadn't gotten that basic need met for far too much of his life. That wound ran so much deeper than hers. Of course, he'd be terrified of not being enough for anyone who mattered. But didn't he know her better than that?

"Why are men so stupid?"

The question had been rather rhetorical, but Scarlett lifted her hands. "It's part of their DNA."

Autumn snorted. "Oh, I like this kid."

Livia couldn't stop the smile. She liked that the girl was a ballbuster. It said a lot about Declan's skill as a parent that she was that comfortable.

Scarlett continued. "Please don't hold it against him. He's been making up for other people's disappointments my whole life."

Livia's heart squeezed again. God, they'd both been hurt. They both deserved someone who could love them exactly how they were. Flaws and all. Sobering, she turned her attention back to Declan. "I wasn't asking for the world. I was asking for communication. Crazy doesn't scare me."

"Well, then you're doing better than me. The crazy regularly scares the shit out of me. Trying to figure out how to manage it, how to wrangle it, how to get through it. But it doesn't scare me half as much as the idea of losing you again."

With another step, he was close enough to touch her, but he didn't.

"I know I screwed up. Twice. After how things went, you probably don't want to give me another shot and sure as hell don't want to risk turning your whole world upside down in pursuit of this. And that's completely fair and understandable. But I'm going to ask for that shot anyway, even though the answer is probably no, because I love you. I've loved you since I was eighteen years old, and if you'll let me, I'll prove I can be better. That I can learn."

He loved her. He *loved her*.

It was the thing she'd needed to hear. The one truth that could make up for all the stress and strain and worry of the past week.

"Do you think she's gonna say yes?" Ginny, Tara's baby sister, whispered in a voice that still carried over the dead silence.

Someone shushed her.

Livia stared at this perfectly imperfect dad, who was trying his best to be everything to everyone. Maybe… Maybe the things he'd done hadn't been *to* her but rather to protect himself. And in, in his way, to protect her as well.

She knew that if she said yes, he'd screw up again, and they'd have to figure out how to make it work. But she could be the person to teach him that he didn't have to show up with every detail already worked out. That part of the journey was sorting the details out together. She knew she'd rather screw things up with him than settle for a shadow of perfect with anyone else. But this wasn't just about them.

Turning to Scarlett, she found the girl waiting with bated breath, hazel eyes so like her father's, bright with curiosity and hope.

Livia began to sign. "Hi. I'm Livia. It's nice to meet you. Are you, by chance, into books?"

The girl's hands flew, even as she spoke. "Books are my favorite."

"Then I guess it's a good thing there's going to be a new bookstore opening where you live."

"There is?" The cautious hope in Declan's tone had her turning back to him.

"When Maggie gets through with me, there

will be. I got accepted into her small business in-cubator program."

Declan's smile spread wide and delighted. "That's amazing! Congratulations."

She could feel his excitement for her and also that he was holding back. Livia appreciated that he didn't make assumptions they'd be jumping back in where they'd left off, but she figured by this point, he'd suffered enough uncertainty.

Stepping into him, she laid her hands on his chest. "There are about eleven thousand details to sort out. Know anybody who can help me with that?"

Relief brightened his eyes as his arms slid around her. "It happens I'm really good with details."

"Good. Let's start with this one." Curling her hands in his sweater, she rose to her toes and kissed him.

EPILOGUE

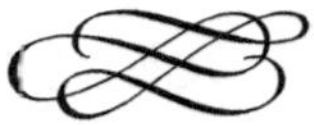

*D*eclan had always loved spring. A time of fresh growth and new beginnings. Longer days and the promise of summer ahead. But he didn't think he'd ever appreciated a new beginning more than this one. The bookstore and wine bar had finally opened its doors, and the grand opening party was in full swing. Everywhere he looked, he saw people he knew, including Livia's brother, Jace, his wife, Tara, and her friends, Autumn and Riley, all of whom had driven up for the opening and were staying at The Misfit Inn. Even her parents had taken a break from their cross-country camper tour to drive up for the occasion.

Autumn, as it turned out, was some kind of

big deal indie author. Her alter ego, Harper Jackson, was making quite a splash in the corner, where she stood in conversation with two other authors who called Eden's Ridge home. Declan hadn't met Ivy Blake Wilkes—a.k.a. Blake Iverson—or Paisley Parish, but he'd certainly heard plenty about both as Livia had ordered stock and discussed signing opportunities with the manic glee only a true book lover could muster.

Tables were tucked into each of the genre sections containing different appetizers, provided by his award-winning chef sister Athena. He spotted Scarlett snagging at least three more of the bacon-wrapped roasted pears. Servers circulated around the room, offering glasses of wine from Temptation Vineyards, along with a sparkling grape juice for the underaged or nondrinkers among the crowd. Declan snagged a glass of wine from a passing tray and surveyed the space, looking beyond the crowd to the haven Livia had made.

She'd kept the exposed brick walls, electing to using shelving to divide up the long room. Instead of feeling chopped up, it felt cozy. Each section felt like its own room, softened with faded rugs and comfy furniture that invited customers to sit down to page through the latest mystery or fall into a fresh romance. The kind of place that you could wander and lose yourself. In the back, surrounded by a perimeter of two- and four-top tables, a long polished bar had been built, and behind it were all the trappings of the tasting room and wine bar. Hope and her brother, Ford, were grinning ear to ear as they poured more wine and answered questions from the patrons standing two and three deep.

"She's in her element, isn't she?"

Declan turned toward Abbey, following her gaze to where Livia was in animated conversation with Juliette Chen, Mick's friend and neighbor that he *still* hadn't made a move on.

"She definitely is."

Livia glowed with happiness, recommending books left and right. Laughing. Making connections and weaving her way into the community.

"I'm thrilled at how everybody's taking to the place. I know all of Maggie's projections were that they would, but you never know until it happens, and I know Liv's had some anxiety over it."

"Well, I'd say she knocked it out of the park," Kyle observed.

"Everybody's excited about the new businesses coming to town. Did you hear about the bakery Jonah Ferguson is opening?" Abbey asked.

Declan frowned. "Sam's brother? Didn't he become a Navy SEAL?"

"He did. But he's out now. Inherited The Right Attitude from his dad and is turning that old eyesore of a bar into a bakery with some buddies."

Kyle laughed. "Trust you to be in the know."

Their infant son started to fuss from the baby sling Abbey had strapped to her chest. She began to bounce, pressing soft kisses to the downy fuzz on baby Brooks' head. "Anyway, it seems like things are going great for all of you."

"Couldn't be much better. Livia's business looks to be a huge success. The house is finally unpacked. I love my job at the Guild. The woman of my dreams was actually willing to take another chance on me. She adores my kid, and the feeling is certainly mutual. I couldn't have asked for anyone better for my daughter or myself. I'm a really lucky man."

Abbey fixed him with a knowing stare. "I'm glad you're aware of it. She *is* my favorite cousin, after all."

Brooks began to crank up louder.

Abbey sighed. "This one's hungry. I'm gonna go sneak back to the office to feed him. Be back."

As his wife strode off, Kyle shifted to stand

shoulder-to-shoulder with Declan so they could both watch Livia. "So, did you ask her yet?"

"Not yet. I wanted to let her get through tonight. But Scarlett and I have plans later."

"Good luck, brother."

Declan didn't really think he'd need it. Not this time. But he said, "Thanks," nonetheless. "I'm gonna go talk to my girl."

He wove his way through the crowd, waiting until Livia had finished her conversation before sliding his arms around her waist from behind. With a happy sigh, she melted back into him.

"Have you eaten anything?" Declan doubted it.

"I've managed a few bites. I've been too busy to eat."

"Things are definitely jumping. Everybody's thrilled."

She spun in his arms and slid hers over his shoulders. "I don't think this could possibly have gone better. I've got different groups booked out for the next *three months,* with more inquiring about event space. The romance book club is already full, and Paisley Parish herself has agreed to come to the first one!"

"That's awesome!" He skimmed the hair back from her radiant face. "I'm really proud of you."

"I'm proud of me, too. Six months ago, I couldn't have imagined being this happy."

"Me neither."

Because he couldn't resist, Declan took her mouth in a soft kiss. He could taste her joy, as effervescent as champagne. Knowing he couldn't keep her to himself, he pulled back. "You have people to greet. I'm gonna make you a plate. But you wanna come over to the house after this is over? Sit down and have some of the wine you totally aren't going to get around to drinking as long as the crowd is here?"

"That's a plan. Thanks, Baby." With one more smacking kiss, she spun away and back into the throng.

Declan met Scarlett's gaze across the room, and he flashed a subtle thumbs up. She grinned and disappeared to enact the second phase of their plan.

* * *

"You sit. I'll pour some wine."

"I won't say no." As Declan disappeared inside the house, Livia sank onto the porch swing and felt every single hour she'd been on her feet. It was overwhelming and exhilarating and utterly exhausting. But worth it. So very worth it.

Scarlett dropped into the Adirondack-style rocker and propped her feet on the porch rail. "Tired?"

"Oh my God, so tired. But so happy, you know?" Having her friends and family come up for the opening meant everything. Of course, they missed her, but they'd been a hundred percent supportive of her move. Her mom, in particular, was delighted at the prospect of inheriting a grandchild. They weren't there yet, but Livia knew they'd get there, eventually. She was here now. They had time.

"You missed out on Athena's appetizers."

Livia smiled at the girl. "I suspect you ate my share for me."

Scarlett grinned. "I plead the fifth."

Declan came back out juggling a couple of glasses and a root beer for Scarlett. He passed out drinks and sank down on the swing beside Livia, toeing it into motion as he always did. Though she was living out at the orchard, she was here almost every day, spending time with her two favorite people, helping with home improvement projects and unpacking. The three of them had bonded over painting, and she'd earned Scarlett's undying gratitude for overruling Declan's original plan to paint the kitchen cabinets white. They'd landed on a soft, misty blue that played well off the fawn-colored walls. There was still more to be done, but things were settled now, with everything out of boxes. The house felt like a home. Livia knew how important that was to Declan.

When he draped an arm along the back of the swing, she slumped against him, more content than she could've imagined as she sipped at the excellent pinot noir and felt the day begin to unwind.

"Since you barely got a chance to eat, I just called in a pizza at Elvira's. It'll be ready in about half an hour."

Livia could have whimpered in gratitude. "You are a god among men. Supreme? With extra mushrooms?"

"Of course."

Scarlett made gagging noises.

"And plain sausage for you."

"Thanks, Dad."

They lapsed into momentary silence, listening to the night music of the mountains. This was her favorite way to end the day, in the quiet with these two people.

"Good day?" Declan ventured.

"Great day," Livia sighed. "Better than I ever could have imagined."

"So you don't regret making this big ass change? Taking the leap to come up here with me?"

Wondering where this tone of uncertainty was coming from, she straightened to look at him. "I could never regret you. Either of you."

His lips curved. "That's good to know. But I think we can make it even better."

"Oh, do you have cheesecake hiding in the fridge?" Now that she'd stopped, her empty stomach was making itself known.

He laughed. "No, but I'll file that away to take care of tomorrow. We have something else in mind."

At that, Scarlett leapt up and disappeared inside.

Livia eyed him with suspicion. "What are you up to?"

"Buying a few moments to do this without an audience." His mouth closed over hers, warm and sure.

Livia melted into him, desire licking through the exhaustion to prove she had a second wind in there somewhere, at least for this. Over the past months, since she'd moved to Eden's Ridge, they'd carved out private time for intimacy, but it was never enough. She craved his kiss and his closeness. But it was so much more than she'd ever thought she'd have with him. She could be patient enough for the rest.

Scarlett came clattering back outside. Livia was pretty sure she'd taken to being as noisy as possible to announce her impending arrival, so they'd be done with the sneaky kissing before she reappeared. Not that she objected to Livia's relationship with her father. The two of them had bonded over mutual love of him and of all things book. Scarlett was, as she had suspected, a delightful kid, and Livia had loved getting to know her better.

The box in her hand was small, wrapped in pretty silver paper with a curling rainbow ribbon. She handed it to Livia.

"What's this?"

"Consider it an opening day present," Declan explained. "The start of the next phase of your life."

Maybe it was something for the shop? Curious, she tugged off the ribbon and ripped the paper so she could open the box inside. Nestled in tissue paper was a key.

"I don't understand."

"It's a key to the house," Scarlett offered.

Confused, Livia looked back and forth between them. "I already have a key to the house."

"We know. This is it. Scarlett snagged it off your keyring."

Scarlett had been digging around in her purse? "Um… why?"

"It didn't make sense to give you another one, but we wanted to give it to you again, as a symbol, because we'd like you to move in with us. Come make a home with us. I mean, you've already been doing that, but we wanted to make it official."

Livia's throat went tight with emotion. "You want me to come live with you?"

That uncertainty was back in his gaze. "I mean, if you're not ready, that's totally cool. We just wanted to put the option on the table—"

Livia fisted a hand in his shirt and cut off his babbling with a fierce kiss. "Yes."

"Yeah?"

"This is exactly what I want. You're exactly what I want. Both of you." Livia reached out an arm to tug Scarlett in, and Declan wrapped them both in a tight embrace. And in the middle of the awkward and perfect group hug with the man and girl she loved, she reflected that wishes did come true in their own time, and she couldn't have come up with a single one that would be better than this.

CHOOSE YOUR NEXT ROMANCE

I HOPE you enjoyed this crossover between the Men of the Misfit Inn and Wishful Romance series! Livia and Declan's story isn't QUITE finished yet. You can grab their bonus epilogue here: https://kaitnolan.com/just-wanted-you-to-know-bonus-epilogue-sign-up/

If this was your first hint taste of Wishful, I've got *great* news for you! There's not one, but TWO whole series for you to binge! It all begins with *To Get Me To You* (Wishful Romance Book 1). Although if you want to jump on to see Riley and Liam, you can do that in *Know Me Well* (Wishful Romance Book 2). Autumn and Judd kick off the spinoff light romantic suspense Wishing for a Hero series with *Make You Feel My Love.*

OTHER BOOKS BY KAIT NOLAN

A complete and up-to-date list of all my books can be found at https://kaitnolan.com.

KILTED HEARTS
SMALL TOWN CONTEMPORARY SCOTTISH ROMANCE

- *Jilting The Kilt* (prequel)
- *Cowboy in a Kilt* (Raleigh and Kyla): January 13
- *Grump in a Kilt* (Malcolm and Charlotte): March 10
- *Playboy in a Kilt* (Connor and Sophie): June
- *Protector in a Kilt* (Ewan and Isobel): August

- *Single Dad in a Kilt* (Hamish and Afton): October

BAD BOY BAKERS
SMALL TOWN MILITARY ROMANCE

- *Rescued By a Bad Boy* (Brax and Mia prequel)
- *Mixed Up With a Marine* (Brax and Mia)
- *Wrapped Up with a Ranger* (Holt and Cayla)
- *Stirred Up by a SEAL* (Jonah and Rachel)
- *Hung Up on the Hacker* (Cash and Hadley)
- *Caught Up with the Captain* (Grey and Rebecca)

RESCUE MY HEART SERIES
SMALL TOWN MILITARY ROMANCE

- *Baby It's Cold Outside* (Ivy and Harrison)
- *What I Like About You* (Laurel and Sebastian)
- *Bad Case of Loving You* (Paisley and Ty prequel)
- *Made For Loving You* (Paisley and Ty)

THE MISFIT INN SERIES
SMALL TOWN FAMILY ROMANCE

- *When You Got A Good Thing* (Kennedy and Xander)
- *Til There Was You* (Misty and Denver)
- *Those Sweet Words* (Pru and Flynn)
- *Stay A Little Longer* (Athena and Logan)
- *Bring It On Home* (Maggie and Porter)

MEN OF THE MISFIT INN
SMALL TOWN SOUTHERN ROMANCE

- *Let It Be Me* (Emerson and Caleb)
- *Our Kind of Love* (Abbey and Kyle)
- *Don't You Wanna Stay* (Deanna and Wyatt)
- *Until We Meet Again* (Samantha and Griffin prequel)
- *Come A Little Closer* (Samantha and Griffin)

WISHFUL ROMANCE SERIES
SMALL TOWN SOUTHERN ROMANCE

- *Once Upon A Coffee* (Avery and Dillon)
- *To Get Me To You* (Cam and Norah)

- *Know Me Well* (Liam and Riley)
- *Be Careful, It's My Heart* (Brody and Tyler)
- *Just For This Moment* (Myles and Piper)
- *Wish I Might* (Reed and Cecily)
- *Turn My World Around* (Tucker and Corinne)
- *Dance Me A Dream* (Jace and Tara)
- *See You Again* (Trey and Sandy)
- *The Christmas Fountain* (Chad and Mary Alice)
- *You Were Meant For Me* (Mitch and Tess)
- *A Lot Like Christmas* (Ryan and Hannah)
- *Dancing Away With My Heart* (Zach and Lexi)

WISHING FOR A HERO SERIES (A WISHFUL SPINOFF SERIES)
SMALL TOWN ROMANTIC SUSPENSE

- *Make You Feel My Love* (Judd and Autumn)
- *Watch Over Me* (Nash and Rowan)
- *Can't Take My Eyes Off You* (Ethan and Miranda)
- *Burn For You* (Sean and Delaney)

MEET CUTE ROMANCE
SMALL TOWN SHORT ROMANCE

- *Once Upon A Snow Day*
- *Once Upon A New Year's Eve*
- *Once Upon An Heirloom*
- *Once Upon A Coffee*
- *Once Upon A Campfire*
- *Once Upon A Rescue*

SUMMER CAMP
CONTEMPORARY ROMANCE

- *Once Upon A Campfire*
- *Second Chance Summer*

ABOUT KAIT

Kait is a Mississippi native, who often swears like a sailor, calls everyone sugar, honey, or darlin', and can wield a bless your heart like a saber or a Snuggie, depending on requirements.

You can find more information on this *USA Today* best selling and RITA ® Award-winning author and her books on her website http://kait nolan.com.

Do you need more small town sass and spark? Sign up for <u>her newsletter</u> to hear about new releases, book deals, and exclusive content!